THE OTHER McCOY

The
OTHER
McCOY

Brian McCabe

MAINSTREAM
PUBLISHING

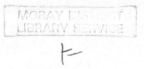
First published in Great Britain in 1990 by
MAINSTREAM PUBLISHING COMPANY (EDINBURGH) LTD
7 Albany Street, Edinburgh EH1 3UG

ISBN 1 85158 305 X (cloth)

British Library Cataloguing in Publication Data
McCabe, Brian
    The other McCoy.
    I. Title
    823'.914 [F]

ISBN 1-85158-305-X

The author would like to thank the Scottish Arts Council and the Canada Council for
a fellowship which gave him time to complete this book.

The publisher gratefully acknowledges the financial assistance of the Scottish Arts
Council in the publication of this volume.

Typeset in 11pt Plantin by Bookworm Typesetting Ltd, Edinburgh.
Printed in Great Britain by Billing and Sons Ltd, Worcester.

For Betty

IT WAS THE last day of the year.

Patrick McCoy, an unemployed comedian, awoke with a bad hangover. The kind of hangover it was difficult not to take personally. He wondered what he'd done to deserve it. It had lasted all the previous day, butting him on the forehead, slipping its chiv into his liver and twisting, booting him in the gut and making his bladder lurch. Now here it was again. He shuddered. He sweated. He held on for dear life to his coat, which was doubling as a blanket because of the freezing cold.

There was that laughter in his head again. Distorted. Like a kind of feedback. It wouldn't go away. It wouldn't leave him alone.

No, stop it, go away.

The screeching laughter paid no attention. Neither did Jinx. She had been pawing at his eyelids to prompt them to open, and now that they had she made the most of treading up and down on his chest determinedly, miaowing in his face sarcastically and staring down at him with her outraged green eyes.

Grim grimalkin.

His mouth did not open properly because of the dryness of his lips, between which there was an unpleasant adhesion, as if he had been licking stamps during his sleep. All those stamps for all those Christmas cards he had not sent, including the one to his widowed mother in Bonnyrigg. Had she sent him one? No.

He couped the cat off his chest as he leaned forward to retch, whereupon she hissed at him spitefully.

Ungrateful feline. He had rescued her en route to the vet's, when his mother had decided the beast should be put out of its misery, on the clear understanding that he would feed her if she

7

took care of the rats, but she had not earned her keep. The rats were still throwing wild parties every night and eating anything they could find, even the soap. Sometimes that was all there was to eat in the place.

The place was terrible. Over the last few years he had been renting one place after another, each more temporary and basic than the last, ending with this one. But maybe it wasn't the end. Maybe the next step would be over the threshold of the hostel for the homeless.

That might even be a step up. McCoy called his present home the shed. That was what it was: a shed. Semple, the owner, had described it as a studio over the phone when McCoy had enquired about it. The man had a way with euphemism. In fact, the shed had been used as a studio by the previous tenant, who had left nothing on the premises but a hoard of empty whisky-bottles and a canvas desecrated with a collage of condoms, so arranged to make the image of a skeletal hand.

'Talk about The New Expressionism,' McCoy had remarked to his friends, who had helped him move his stuff in, 'If I had something like that to express, I'd take up alcoholism instead.'

'Many have,' John Grogan had replied, sadly. Then: 'At least they're used. Think of all that life in there –'

They had turned to Paul Haggerty for his professional opinion on the matter, he being an aspiring painter of sorts himself. Haggerty shook his head and said nothing, angrily.

'It's an image of the eighties,' MacRae had said, gloomily. 'Mind you, it might make no a bad book cover.'

MacRae was the son of a minister from Aberdeen and had published some poetry, and though he had never actually published a book of it, he was always talking about a book that would surely come out soon and the question of what the cover should show was never far from his thoughts. McCoy and Grogan pulled his leg about it mercilessly:

'Aye, *The Wee Free Dae-it-yersel Guide To Safer Sex*,' McCoy had teased. 'A slim volume. A limited edition of one. For the Elect only.'

'Better make it a trilogy for us Catholics, eh Pat?' Grogan had elaborated, 'we're cursed with the holy pack of three.'

'Call it *Holey Condoms: The Catholic Compromise*,' McCoy had added.

8

Laughter.

Now McCoy's empty whisky bottles had doubled the previous tenant's hoard and his own joke about alcoholism had turned against him. All his jokes had a knack of turning against him in the end. The one about the holey condoms was one he could have done without: the last one he'd used with Yvonne had burst.

That was a while ago now. After the pub. At her place. Always her place. The shed made her depressed.

'It's got character. It's solid. It's got potential,' he'd said to her, the first time he'd brought her here. She had looked at him askance and rolled her big dark eyes and said:

'It's got about as much character as a nissen hut. It's about as solid as a cardboard box in a nuclear holocaust. And as for potential, it's a potential health-hazard, if you ask me. My place, or forget it.'

After a half-hearted attempt to fix the cistern, he had given up any attempt at home improvements, sensing the futility of the enterprise: a sow's ear was a sow's ear. The shed had done more to him than he had done to it.

The thing with Yvonne had got steadily worse since the day he'd moved in. She had tried to dissuade him, talked about living together, hinted that there was room for him at her place. But he had been unwilling to commit himself to co-habitation. It would complicate his already fractious relationship with the D.H.S.S. And money. Money was in there somewhere as well, it had become an issue between them – the fact that she earned it and he didn't. He could imagine how the money-tension might develop if they lived together. Still, he had to admit that she'd eased off on that score lately. The time to live together had come, and very soon it would have come and gone.

Let her not be with child. Not yet. Not now. Not like this.

In the meantime the shed was coming between them: she refused to stay the night in a shed infested with rats, and though McCoy could not blame her for that, he sometimes did.

The shed had never been intended for human habitation, constructed as it was of corrugated iron and wood, raised from the overgrown ground in which it sat by a narrow foundation of brick and hidden from the mews in which it was situated by a high wall topped with, of all things, broken glass. Intruders would have run a mile. From the door in this wall a wooden staircase

9

led to the door of the shed, then turned and led further down to one of the last outside water closets in Scotland and the cellar of an adjacent tenement building, which boasted a sink and so served as McCoy's kitchen. He was the only person he knew with an outside kitchen. He didn't like to think about that kitchen down there. Dank. The word was dank. It smelled foostie and behind the foostiness lurked the more serious smell of the rats.

Go and sort them out, Jinx, or go.

She marched up and down on his chest and miaowed in his face again. Although he was still hungover and barely awake, he couldn't resist imitating her venomous expression and hoarse miaow. It had always been a habit of his – some had called it a gift, others a weakness – to imitate people, animals and sometimes even politicians. So McCoy stared back at the cat and uttered a parched impersonation of her starved miaow, whereupon she disclosed her claws and rasped her tongue against his unshaven chin.

Abrasive, yes, certainly, but abrasive doesn't quite express the, ah . . . cat's-tongue quality of the humour . . .

This in the intonation of a critic he had heard once on radio, on a programme to do with the arts and entertainments in Scotland. Hadn't the same critic described one or two of his own routines as promising? Hadn't he also said that McCoy had 'presence' and 'unlimited potential'?

Oh yes, at the time he had sat there at the radio savouring the praise. Now the critic's words echoed in his mind, with the horrible interference of the laughter, as a snide insult. That patronising 'promising'. Presence. Now there was a thing to conjure with. What the hell was it? Didn't everybody have it? What he felt up there was something different. What he felt was the overcoat feeling. Like being an overcoat. Like being tried on by somebody else. What he felt up there was absence. And 'potential' had long since ceased to feel like a pat on the head.

And wasn't that why he did it, why he had always done it? Stood up in godforsaken church halls on the Fringe, sweating his guts out trying to wring a laugh out of the bastards and for what? A pat on the head! He's a grown man, but he still needs a pat on the head! Still got unlimited potential!

'About as much potential as a cardboard Nissen hut in a nuclear holocaust. . .' so Yvonne's words echoed and distorted in his hungover brain as McCoy itched and sweated and retched his way in and out of consciousness.

If only the wild laughter inside would go away. It was out of some dark place inside him. Out of control. Out of order.

The truth was a different story. He was unemployed. He was unmarried. He was unknown. There were too many uns in his life. Also, he was skint. In order to make ends nearly meet he had recently pawned the suit he kept for his rare appearances in public, and with the proceeds had bought a hand-drill and a quantity of spy-holes. He had been hoofing it round the doors of Edinburgh since then, offering to fit the bloody things at an economical rate.

What seems at first sight to be an inspiration, an ideal way of supporting the Income Support, transpires to become a kind of gruelling ritual of self-abasement.

That critic again. Switch him off.

Three days ago, Christmas or not, a letter had come from Semple saying if his rent arrears weren't paid by the end of December, he would evict him. 'I will get you evicted out of there,' had been his landlord's exact words, and McCoy knew from experience that the threatened eviction would not be a legal process: a couple of heavies would arrive at the door, as they had once before when the rent was late. Either that or he'd come home one day from a hard day selling holes to find the lock changed and a pitiful bundle of his naked belongings strewn over the cobbled ground of the mews. No doubt Jinx would abandon the sinking ship.

Christ no, Semple. Don't change the lock. Don't put my stuff out in the street. I am a humble artist on the brink of national acclaim.

He had to get up. He had to get out there and sell some holes. But there was something else, something good, something to set against all this, something that made life worth living . . . On the brink of national acclaim.

Of course, tonight was the night: his debut t.v. appearance. On *The Hogmanay Show*. A five-minute spot. Just before the bells, the producer had said, and had invited him to a party at his place to watch it. There would be a few t.v. people there, without a doubt. This year, the Tron was definitely out. He would make sure he was somewhere where he could watch himself. A lot of people

11

watched *The Hogmanay Show*. It was a start. It was *the* start. It could lead to other work. It had to. Everyone in The Steamies – the scheme of flat-roofed, centrally heated Council Houses in Bonnyrigg where he had grown up – would be sitting there glued to their sets. Mrs Payne upstairs, Mr and Mrs Schmidt next door. His mother. More, all over Scotland people would be watching. Forget the counter-clerk in the D.H.S.S. If he hauled him in for an interrogation, he would tell him the truth: he hadn't been paid for it yet, even though the show had been recorded in October.

Cut that canned laughter.

Jinx clawed at his neck. McCoy retaliated: he grabbed her by the scruff of her fur and threw her to the floor. He cried out, because she had taken some of his neck with her, and now the hangover closed in for another go at him. He leaned over the side of the bed and retched.

No, stop it, don't. I was only young once.

Though he retched doggedly there was little to show for it but a thin apology of milkish bile, which tasted of single fish.

He watched the cat as she crept with measured stealth around the bed, circled the colourless little pool of anonymous fluid, sniffed at it gingerly and declined.

Ya wan't rough house . . . that's what ya get.

Brando in *A Streetcar Named Desire* talking to Vivienne Leigh as Blanche.

When you move in here, we make a deal Jinx. The deal was, I feed you, you take care of the rats. But you don't take care of no rats. You sit around on that fat, furry ass and eat my food and drink my drink . . .

Too easy.

The cat, seeming to sense that food was being discussed, responded with the grievance of her miaow.

He retched again.

From now on lemonade and lime. Not a drop this side of the grave. Not until the day I die.

OUT OF HABIT, Yvonne flung the downy aside and sat up in bed as soon as she woke up. Then she remembered it was the holidays and started to fall back into sleep again, but just as her head touched the pillow the whole swooning movement brought the image of the bridge back, and the body falling. Sometimes he tumbled and sometimes he somersaulted. This time he spread his arms wide. His coat flapped like the ragged wings of a wounded bird.

She covered her eyes with her hands but the bird kept flapping its big black wings as it hurtled towards the ground.

Fly away, big black bird.

Her head hurt from the half-bottle of gin she'd consumed alone, with determination, last night, after Helen had phoned and told her.

It had happened after the party, after she'd stormed out and left him. He'd been pissed as a newt. On the way home, he'd thrown himself off the Dean Bridge.

Her first reaction to the news was an obscure anger towards him, as if to die young was somehow typical of him – and it was typical of him. He was always slipping off early when she took him to a teachers' do, making his elaborate excuses and escaping to the pub before she knew it. It had always infuriated her the way he made himself elusive when she needed him. And now, at New Year of all times, it was as if he'd made himself scarce on purpose, to spite her.

She grabbed a pillow and threw it at his photograph on top of the bookcase. It knocked over the vase full of paintbrushes, but McCoy went on staring into the sky with infuriating nonchalance. She had taken it soon after they'd met. It showed him leaning against a pillar of the Dean Bridge and looking up . . . trust it to be the very bridge. Had he been contemplating it even then? She felt the urge to cry again but stopped herself in time. Her eyelids still felt swollen from last night. She stood up abruptly, winced at the pain behind her eyes and stamped her way over the floor, kicking the fallen pillow as she went. She crossed her arms over her breasts and rubbed her hands up and down her goosefleshed arms, shuddering with a kind of angry satisfaction, as if this physical feeling of being cold vindicated what she was feeling inside. She stood still for a moment, staring at the dim image of herself naked in the long mirror as if at a stranger, shuddering as the cold air of the morning crept over her flesh like the breath of a fresh ghost.

She tugged her dressing gown from its hanger on the rail and wrapped it round herself, then went through to the kitchen and started to make some coffee.

While it was brewing she looked out of her kitchen window. It was just beginning to get light. The snowflakes looked dark against the sky. When she did poetry with the fifth year, in some poem the snow had been compared to a shroud. It was a cliché. Even now, to her, when the snow bloody well should look like a shroud, it didn't. It didn't look like anything. It was just snow. How she had loved to feel it as a girl, the cold crispness of it in her hand. That was a cliché as well, but it was one no one knew about. It was her own, private cliché. And she still loved it, still wanted to go out in it and feel its light touch on her skin. She could still do that, that wasn't anything to do with him, she could still go for a walk in the snow. And everything else, she could still go on doing everything else she did. Everything except anything she did with him.

What did she do with him?

They hadn't been getting on well lately, but that didn't mean anything. The row they'd had seemed petty, it couldn't be that. Or could it? She knew him well enough to know that there was the other McCoy, the one he called the public one – 'the one that can't stay out of the pub . . .' – the one that needed the laughter and the applause. It didn't matter who the audience was – she had had to be it often enough to know that. An audience of one.

14

Maybe it had been the other McCoy, not the real one, not the one who watched people and listened to people. He had to watch them and listen to them to be able to mimic them. It was the watching, listening one she loved, not the other one.

Something must have made him do it, something he hadn't told her about. He hadn't been confiding in her lately. She hadn't been confiding in him much either. Something was coming between them. Teaching. The fact that she was a teacher. That must be what it was. It was screwing up everything else. Why shouldn't it screw up her relationship as well?

He had an inferiority complex and that didn't help. A chip on his shoulder about his education, or lack of it. He was always making her feel guilty about having gone to university, being qualified as a teacher and having more money than him.

Sometimes she thought it came down to a choice: jack in the job, or jack in him. Some choice. The kind of choice that shouldn't happen, the kind of choice that was no choice at all.

But none of that could explain it. His money problems? They were nothing new, if anything he felt insecure without them. She had once told him that without his constant struggle to scrape together enough money to get drunk he'd be lost, he wouldn't know what to do, he'd have a real problem.

The kind of problem I could do with, he'd said, in somebody else's voice.

She poured the coffee into a mug, moved through to the living room and sat down at the coffee table. She looked at the telephone with disgust. Yesterday she'd had calls from Paul Haggerty, Cathy, Hugh Mitchell, Tony McTaggart, all with messages of sympathy and condolence. Haggerty's had taken the longest, and he'd said the least. It was amazing how silent he could be, even on the phone. Grogan had been the last, then she'd left the phone off the hook, cried again and gone out to buy the gin. She must get in touch with his mother. She didn't know her address or phone number. All she knew was that she lived in Bonnyrigg, in a place he called The Steamies. She had spent a few hours trying to find the address or the number, but it was typical of him that none of his friends knew. And neither did she. There was something all wrong about that. And if she did find it, what would she say to her? The good news is you're going to be a granny, the bad news is, your son's dead. But maybe she'd have been told about

15

it already. His death. It was like that. It was his. He had made an act of it. Not something that happened to you. Something you did.

She might not be. She had been later than this before. She felt nauseous, but maybe that was just the gin. She might not be. But if she was, what would she do? When he was alive, the idea of getting pregnant and having his child had seemed unlikely. Even if he'd committed himself to it. Even if he'd moved in, there would be problems. The place would be okay for six months but they'd have to find somewhere bigger. She'd have to go back to teaching as soon as she could, unless he got a job. That's how she'd been thinking about it until yesterday, but now that he was dead, the idea of having his child seemed more viable. Maybe she could handle that – if she didn't have to handle him as well.

Helen had been vague about some things. Had he left the party on his own? Had he said anything before he'd left? Where was the body? When was the funeral? All those things Grogan had wanted to know, and though at the time she had felt that it would somehow cheapen something to know these things, now she saw Grogan's point.

She must get a paper for the report. It would be an ordeal to read it, but she wanted the ordeal. It might help her to realise what had actually happened and she was not one to turn away from the truth. She would meet it face to face.

She remembered someone saying something in a play she had read about grief. The trouble with grief was that it didn't last. Something like that. She hadn't started yet. She hadn't found it yet. She had started to look for it, and in the process of looking had started to feel it, but she knew that it would have to burst in on her soon.

Maybe when she read the report in the paper. Or when she saw the body, or felt it, felt the cold that was different from any other cold because it was final, it was absolute, a final and absolute absence. Or at the funeral, when his coffin was lowered slowly into the narrow, deep, obscene trench in the earth. Or maybe at midnight, when his ghost was due to appear on *The Hogmanay Show*. The thought made her put her coffee down hastily. She opened her eyes wide and stared at the dark screen of the television. To watch him doing his routine to a studio audience . . . it was unbearable but inescapable. She would have

16

to sit through it, she would have to record it and sit through it again and again, unless she was strong enough not to.

She was strong enough not to.

She had to do something. She needed a course of action. She needed a space to think in, needed to clear her head, needed to get out.

She took her coffee through to the bedroom and started to rummage among the clothes on the rack for something to put on. Her hand found the black dress she'd been wearing when she'd met him and she looked again at the photograph of him under the bridge. She felt the urge to cry again but stopped herself by biting her bottom lip until it hurt.

She threw the dress on the bed.

Fly away, big black bird.

He TURNED OVER in bed and heard a noise somewhere low in his own throat. The death rattle. As if he had died or something inside of him had died, some beautiful, useless possibility he had until now always clung to. To be somebody, somebody else, somebody not himself.

And it was like that. When he was good. As if he'd given himself the slip and stepped inside the other McCoy, the one that wasn't him, the one he was impersonating.

He used it to judge his performances. That weird feeling that was like being an overcoat. An overcoat. And somebody was trying you on. It was usually reliable, the overcoat feeling, because when he felt it the audience felt it as well: the Other McCoy.

Demonic laughter.

A witch can't come under her own spell. A priest can't hear his own confession. A comedian can't laugh at his own joke.

But were they laughing in recognition of the Other? Was it not themselves they recognised? But it could be that recognition was the wrong name for it altogether, that recognition had nothing to do with it. It could be that it had no name, and if it had no name, it could be that it didn't exist, that he had always just imagined it. But even if he had always just imagined it, he still felt it. The eerie feeling of being the Other, of being tried on like an overcoat . . . And even after, when he came off, he sometimes felt dazed. There was a lingering unease, a physical queasiness complicated by the need to drink, the need to obliterate – obliterate what? Himself, or the traces of the Other?

After the show, if he'd been good, he would feel high, with a nervous energy it was difficult to dispel, and he'd jabber away

18

to somebody about anything at all. It didn't matter who it was. Somebody from the audience, somebody backstage, the guy counting the door-take, the janny waiting to lock up the building, a barmaid, a drunk. As long as they were there talking to him or listening to him he felt reassured – but reassured about what? That he was there, that he was still there, that the Other hadn't stolen him away. But sometimes it was as if a piece of him had been stolen away, or that he'd given a piece of himself away, and the worst thing about it was that he didn't know which piece it was, and didn't know what he was left with, and had no notion of who had stolen it – the audience, or the Other?

These doubts lingered all the more if he hadn't been good. Then there was the compulsion to drink, and the strange sensations of queasiness and anxiety and the need to phone somebody – Yvonne, Grogan, Haggerty, MacRae, anybody who hadn't seen him die out there tonight. Still he'd be haunted by the lines he'd mistimed, the gestures that hadn't quite come off, especially if he was on his own.

The restlessness of the audience was behind him but it was still there, chasing him all the way along the street to the nearest pub to drown his sorrows. That was what was worst, that feeling that you were on your own and that you had somehow betrayed yourself. Or the Other.

– Who are you?

My own worst enemy.

– Stand in line with others.

Get your voices out of my head.

The first time he'd met Yvonne, he'd done his father on stage. In a working man's club in Denny, between the local band battering out 'The Green Green Grass of Home' and the bingo.

The routine about the day his father and Jimmy McGeechan, his father's drinking crony, took him to Portobello on the Glasgow Holiday. His father telling him that McGeechan was the devil and if he didn't behave himself he'd take him to hell on the way home.

How many wee laddies have ye in Hell the now, Jimmy?

Aw . . . Abbubububbout t-en.

McGeechan had been good to do, with his stutter and his chain smoking and his evasive reluctance to play the role of the devil that had been thrust on him.

19

But he had really been the devil for the boy McCoy, filling the living-room in The Steamies with blue smoke. The devil could blow smoke-rings. He could even make it come out of his ears. The devil drove a sardine tin.

It needed a lot of mime, a lot of body movement and comic posture about going down the Royal Mile in McGeechan's sardine tin. Arriving at Portobello and being told to hold on to the railings outside that pub on the prom while they went in and got pissed: 'Haud ontae they railins or else ye'll gawn straight tae hell, that right Jimmy?' The devil's devilish smile. Then the painful comedy of holding on to those railings there and not letting go. And the stuff about the Scottish bathing habits. Being sent out on the *Skylark* and thinking that you'd been sent away to some far off place and that the Portobello coastline, when the boat had turned round to come back in, was somewhere else and that you were never going to see your daddy again. Getting taken to the open-air pool – 'There was the Scottish idea of a swimmin pool, just open the door and let the bloody sea in!' And so on, right through to the comedy of being shoved into a back room of a pub on the way home and drinking lemonade and eating crisps with all the other kids whose dads were getting pissed.

– Which yin's your daddy?

– That's him sittin in the corner wi the divvel.

– He's no the divvel.

– Aye he is.

– Where's his hoarns then?

– Under his hair. He can make the smoke come oot his ears.

There was as much tragedy in it as comedy. It was all in the way it was done. It was all true, or at least, at one time he had thought it was true, before he'd made it into a routine. It had all happened to him and they liked it in the Denny Working Man's Club, in fact they were lapping it all up, it was one of his best performances . . . but then at a certain point when he was imitating his father it had happened, he had given himself the slip and stepped into the Other, and the audience had come together for the first time because although they didn't know the father they suddenly sensed that it was the father before them and not the son, and in this father they recognised all their fathers and laughed as one. And he had felt suddenly angry at them

20

for laughing. And even when he had come off and was hearing somebody telling him that he'd been very good and would he be interested in coming to the B.P. dinner-dance in Grangemouth, he still felt angry and resentful with the audience, but couldn't tell whether it was his own anger he was feeling, or his father's.

He didn't shake it off until the anger made his arm jump suddenly, in a spasm of memory, knocking a glass off the table. The movement was his father's. It was exactly how he would have knocked over a glass by accident. And suddenly he saw a part of his father he had never seen before. Not the anger he'd let out but the anger he'd kept in, the anger that made him accidentally knock over a glass with a sudden movement of the hand. That gesture had betrayed him.

The glass shattered on the floor. Someone clapped. There was something between a cheer and a groan.

Then a voice said: 'It looked like you meant that.'

He looked across the table at her. She was smiling, but her eyes were dark and serious. She was wearing a black dress, smoking a cigarette. She looked good.

He apologised and went straight to the bar to buy her another. She was sitting with her father, so he bought the old man a pint as well.

I didn't mean it to be like that, Yvonne. Our meeting was an accident, but once the accident had happened, there was no going back for either of us.

He had never attempted to mimic his father again.

It didn't do to think about it too much. The business of imitating somebody else was eerie. Even if you did it well there was always a point after when you felt that it had all been a cheap trick, a sham, that you were a charlatan who'd sold your soul to Jimmy McGeechan, to the devil, to the Other McCoy.

It was always the other person's faults you had to go for, their weaknesses. And so you got into the habit of looking at everyone for their faults and their weaknesses, and that wasn't a good way to look at people, was it? Of course it wasn't. Maybe that's why he had stopped himself the minute he'd found himself starting to look at Yvonne like that, sensing by some performer's instinct that it would be funny to do her but at the same time dangerous. Any imitation of someone you loved had to be a cheap imitation. That's what it was all about and it wasn't good for anybody, it was not healthy. It was these few shreds of the Other you stepped into, not the whole person, but when you were good you managed to make the few shreds look and sound and feel like the whole person – and wasn't that just like what happened in a relationship? You got to know different bits of the Other, but not the whole person. Then the pieces broke up into other pieces, until you looked at the Other and thought, 'I thought I knew her.' Wasn't that what would happen with Yvonne?

Supposing she was pregnant. The thought brought the sweat to his brow but even so, just supposing. And she decides to go ahead and have it. Jesus Christ, she just might. And even if they managed to live together as the poor little bastard's parents, what did he have to offer the child? At least his own father had been working in the pit. At least they'd had a home they could call their own, even if it wasn't. Not a rat-infested shed.

Yvonne, we are going to live in a place I know away from the dreary stresses and niggling uncertainties of our lives here. A place where you still don't have to lock your door at night and nobody needs to have a spy-hole. There is a front door and a back door, a coal bunker and a drying green, a place where people have greenhouses and grow tomatoes and use their communal verandahs to park the pram, the motorbike and the disused cooker, where the children gambol happily on the bings of the derelict coal-mines and the overgrown railway and the devil makes smoke come out of his ears and drives a sardine tin. A place where the houses have flat roofs, no chimneys and metal framed windows. Yes Yvonne, and the great thing about them is that they're centrally heated straight from the furnaces of Hell. It'll be dead handy for your work at the school as well. You won't be imported from the city any longer like all the other teachers who work there, you'll be living there in the community, you'll be a respected member of Hell, you'll understand the damned better and they'll understand you better. Yvonne, I'm talking about the first centrally heated scheme of council houses to be built in Scotland, circa 1940, yes Yvonne, I want you to come with me now to make a new life for ourselves in the past, in The Steamies of Hell.

What did he have to offer? A shed. No neighbours with the same leaky radiators as you. No job. Scarce prospects. A mixed bunch of friends and aquaintances. No community. No social fabric.

Maybe that was why he needed to be somebody, somebody else, somebody *not himself*, and maybe that was why he imitated other people . . . Not like an actor, no. His need was different.

A new personality, sir? Certainly, sir. This is the National Health Range, these over here are a little more expensive.

Canned laughter. Can it.

Why do I do it?

The name he was cursed with at birth. McCoy. How sick he was of all those wise-crackers who would say, when he was introduced to them, 'McCoy? The real one?'

No. The other one.

Restless silence. A low-toned comment. A cough.

His first name had done nothing to mitigate the crime of the surname. Patrick. Pat. Paddy. People always assumed he was Irish through and through and were frequently disappointed to discover that he was not. Sometimes he didn't disabuse them of their notion, but affected a plausible lilt. On my father's side, to be sure.

And to be sure it was true. At least, his father had always made something of being Irish, or at any rate partly Irish on his own father's side, so that naturally he would choose his son the name of Pat to go with the McCoy. But what about his older brother, Mike? Mike, Michael – it wasn't nearly so bad, somehow. He wondered if Michael, now married with three kids and working in Crawley as a social worker, had gone through life being ribbed about his surname too. Even if he had, his first name must have been a consolation. Pat, Paddy, Patrick, on the other hand . . . If only he'd been Mike McCoy, or John McCoy, or some other McCoy.

He was an imitation Irishman.

Dad, what possessed you to name me thus?

As he drifted back into sleep, he thought of his father coming home on a Saturday night in a condition of drunken grandeur: arms outstretched as if to embrace the whole household, or more, the entire continent of Ireland herself, so he staggers with a swagger through the dim closing-time streets of The Steamies, singing a romantic or political song, or one that is a bit of them both, which though it may very well have originated in the West

23

Midlands of England sounds thoroughly Irish nevertheless the way he sings it, that is to say from the corner of his mouth not otherwise engaged with the business of the cigarette, trying one or two of the doors along the street before he hits upon the one which is his. The boy McCoy runs to meet him at the door, opens it, over the threshold then steps John McCoy, his coat and his flies liberally unbuttoned, his beaming face as flushed and shining as a roasted ham, his blue eyes alit from within by a vision of the colleens of Donegal, holding aloft his prize and his glory: a family-size steak pie, won at the dominoes. So the hunter returns, slipping a don't-tell-your-mother half-crown into his son's hot palm and allowing him to lead him to the living-room and his armchair, the one with the many cigarette burns along its arms and the racing section stuffed behind the cushion, whereupon follow the declarations of Irish blood and the tea and sandwiches provided by his good wife. A woman of no nonsense, Mary McCoy had no time for her husband's Irish brand of it, though there were plaques with shamrocks on the living-room walls to attest to the time she had allowed herself to be cajoled into a fortnight's holiday in Dublin.

As the memory lurched into a dream, McCoy again steps on to the stage of the living-room carpet and gets ready to do his routine for his parents, who are sitting on the setee that hasn't been paid for yet with their coats on and their suitcases packed ready. The whole scene is frozen, like a still from a film. A few of the neighbours have come in for the leavetaking: there is Mrs Payne from upstairs, standing at the sideboard, wearing the kind of cross-over pinny that seems to wrap around everything at least once, even her stupendous breasts. She looks as if she has been crying and will cry again soon.

Her puffed, saddened face. Of course, it's only a few weeks since her husband Dan dropped dead at the oatcake factory. The boy McCoy has not mourned his passing. He had avoided Dan Payne since the time he'd bullied him into admitting that he wasn't always good at school and smacked him across the hand for it. The boy McCoy and his sister Frances went upstairs to see her more often since she'd become a widow. She owned a radiogramme and a long-playing record of the soundrack of *Rawhide*, as well as a television with a 42-inch screen. Sometimes she would amuse them by doing handstands, despite her wheezing bulk, against the living-room wall while the music whipcrackawayed on the radiogramme, and the boy McCoy would take the opportunity to study, when her dress fell over her face, her capacious and complex underwear, which seemed to involve so many frills, catches, buttons, buckles and ribbons. Without her husband, she had trouble getting her boys, Paul and Brian, to go to bed, and the boy McCoy had once seen the columns of threepenny bits she had put by each of their beds in an attempt to bribe them to sleep. The Payne children ate raw sausages and soggy biscuits and filled empty milkbottles with their urine and played *Rawhide* at full volume when their mother was out at the shops.

There by the window, watching out for the taxi, is Mrs Schmidt, the German woman from next door, in a similar but smarter-looking wrap-around pinny than Mrs Payne's. She wears her black hair up in a bun and has the trace of a German moustache above her wide German lips. Mrs Schmidt is married to a lean, frowning, mean-faced man who has his black German hair cut in a very short crew-cut and rides a German velocopede to his work in the Carpet Factory. Being German, he beats her mercilessly, so the story goes, and there are times when she seeks refuge in the McCoy household to cry and tell her neighbours the woeful story of her life in great guttural German sobs and screeches.

His sisters, Mary and Frances, are there as well and his brother Mike is looking in the mirror and combing his hair. The audience is there for him, and the boy McCoy knows that he must make the most of it now, for who knows when the next audience will come along? But as he is about to go into his impersonation of Andy Stewart imitating Elvis, Mrs Schmidt turns from the window and says, 'It eez here' and he feels the audience slip away as the room bustles with the palaver of his parents' leavetaking.

Again he runs out into the sunlit street of The Steamies, sees those flat-roofed houses with the communal verandahs and the metal windows, feels the rutted concrete of the road through the worn soles of his gymshoes and hears the shuddering engine of the taxi-cab come to take his Ma and Da to Dublin. Again he feels afraid of it, for in the world of The Steamies in the mid-fifties, a taxi has some of the same ominous magic of the Black Maria and the hearse. Now his mouth is being wiped with the licked corner of a handkerchief, there is the bright red taste of his mother's lipstick, and everyone is shouting good luck and waving as the taxi draws away from the kerb and he is running after it, the tears streaming from his eyes. Oh but now Frances, his older sister, has caught him and has taken him inside to give him a bath in the sink and smack the back of his hand when he touches his willie . . . At last, a vestige of moral order will come to the McCoy household now that the parents are away.

(The only photograph they would bring home from holiday was taken by a street photographer and showed John McCoy dressed in a blazer, a rolled up racing section held at his shoulder like the handle of a rifle, scowling at the camera, the wind lifting the last of his thinned hair, and his headscarfed wife on his arm, smiling the way she always smiled in photographs, her wide-open eyes magnified by the thick lenses of her glasses. So John McCoy and his good wife Mary stood arm-in-arm to be photographed before the mundane facade of a jeweller's shop in Dublin bearing their name, McCoy's, as if the conjunction of the name with riches in the photograph might magically bring about the same conjunction in life.)

((It did not.))

THE CHATTERING OF his teeth woke him up. He pulled the blankets up around his chin to try to shield his face from the persecuting cold of the winter and Scotland and the shed. Even his eyes felt cold. When he closed them, it felt as if someone had placed two cold pennies on them, coins colder than the corpse itself. When he opened them, it made things no better: the cold had moved into the shed.

His odds and ends of furniture looked as if they felt it too, crouching in the corners and huddling around the bed like a brood of petrified beasts. The worn strip of carpet beside his bed seemed to shrink from the expanses of icy linoleum on either side of it. What a pitiful bit of rug it was, with its weave showing through those threadbare roses. It was certainly time to return it to the skip from which it had come. Everything looked cold in the shed, as if steeped in the cold, as if he was wearing glasses made of ice.

He looked at the window. It was getting light but the light was dull. He could see the snowflakes whirling in the pool of yellow light from the streetlamp in the mews. He tried to follow the path of one of them, but it made him dizzy to watch it, as if he himself was falling . . .

'And as I watched I realised that every one of us is like that wee snowflake, whirled and spun in the senseless hurly-burly of the modern world as we know it today, and we all get dizzy. And like that wee snowflake, every one of us has his brief illumination in the yellow light from the streetlamp, before plunging into the darkness below. And every one of us is watched. Even here in Scotland, or maybe I should say, *especially* here in Scotland. Only the other day, I was walking through the snow, alongside

27

a very famous golf course in St Andrews, when my eight-year-old grand-daughter said to me, "Grand-dad, where does the wind come from?" Well, as you can probably see for yourselves, I'm no a meteorologist. So I licked my finger and held it up to see which direction the wind was coming from, the way people do, and I said to her: Leuchars. That's one of our American bases, just north of St Andrews, by the way . . .'

He liked a good *Late Call*, but the thought of the whirling snow was making his head reel, so that he had to grip the bed and hold on. The bed was a raft, apparently, and under it there was the sea. What had happened to the curtains? Apparently they had capsized. Apparently the shed had been dashed against the rocks during the night and now here he was, the survivor, washed up and gasping for breath, clinging to the purulent seaweed of his bedclothes.

He dimly remembered accidentally wrenching the curtains from their rail the night before yesterday's all-day hangover, having come home – like father like son – in a condition of drunken grandeur. Where had he been?

Let me not remember any of it.

A party. He had been at a party. Whose party? To celebrate what? Isolated moments of it began to surface in his memory, like bits of a home-made video.

The look of resignation on Ian MacRae's face as Helen Aitken took him up to dance. Cathy Lyon interrupting her dance with Graham Pearson to say something to Paul Haggerty. Yvonne putting on her coat, mouthing a hurt curse at him, telling him never to darken her door again and storming out into the night. Had they gone to the party together? No. He had said something or done something to upset her, but what? He couldn't remember. Had he run after her, down the stair, out into the street, catching her by the arm and wrapping her in his arms and pleading, 'Come on now, Yvonne, I didn't mean that. Honest. I'm sorry and it's late, so let's go back to your place for some tea, some toast, the late night movie and bed –'?

He had not.

Instead he'd lingered at the party and had got seriously pissed. A typical teacher's party with bowls of crisps on the sideboard and conversations about politics in the queue for the toilet. He'd stayed in that hell-hole, with the hard-core of pub-crawling, party-going singles Ian MacRae liked to call the Out-crowd, because they were always planning excursions, parties and piss-ups, always going out, and because they were too old to be an in-crowd, and because although he mixed with them, MacRae liked to think that he wasn't one of them.

The Out-crowd were an uneasy mixture of McCoy's friends, that assorted band of ne'er-do-wells, and Yvonne's, who were mostly teachers from the school she worked in. His friends envied hers their security and their salaries; hers envied his their lack of commitment, their freedom. What they had in common was that they had reached the point where they were starting to panic about their lives.

Look at Yvonne and her pal Cathy Lyon. They'd both hit the critical thirty-four last year. Only a year to get pregnant in before they'd be termed Geriatric Mothers. Yvonne was with McCoy, but not living-with. Cathy Lyon was between men, swithering between Graham Pearson the History teacher and the laconic Paul Haggerty, an unemployed painter friend of MacRae's. Helen Aitken was between men as well, having exhausted a succession of them, and she'd been warming up MacRae at the party the other night. Had Grogan been there? No. Tony McTaggart, the drama teacher, the one who was having an open house tonight – he'd been there, and as they were draining the dregs and standing around in the kitchen, Tony had egged him on: Do Mitch, he'd said. Of course, Hugh Mitchell – it had been his going away party. And he'd walked into the kitchen just at that moment, as if answering to his name.

McCoy wasn't sure about him, but could never make up his mind whether this was because Yvonne kept using him as an example of things McCoy was not – an athletic, well-dressed, gainfully employed, reliable car-owner – or because he was a gym teacher.

More than once he'd suspected that her weekly workout at the Tone Up Your Body Evening Class might become a preamble to Sex On The Wallbars. Did any of that make him think twice about mimicking him? No, he went ahead and did Hugh Mitchell to a T, right down to his habit of flexing his jaw-muscle and raising his eyebrows before speaking in his slow, embarrassed, one-word-at-a-time way, rising up and down on the balls of his feet the way gym teachers do. Oh Christ it had all been there,

29

magnified into high relief by his callous impersonation. Even Hugh Mitchell had flushed and joined in with the laughter and the applause. Then someone had said: 'Eh . . . where's Yvonne?'

No doubt he'd come home by instinct, the poor man's taxi.

But that wasn't all. There was something worse. On the way home, he had met somebody. They had stood under a streetlamp, talking. She'd given him a cigarette. He'd said . . . he'd told her some terrible lie. She'd believed it, believed him . . .

Who? What? Why?

Had he tried to get off with a complete stranger?

He had the feeling it was something worse than that.

Oh no.

He groaned and hid his head under the covers for shame of what he could remember and for fear of what he couldn't. Something trailed from a corner of his mouth and made a damp stain on his pillow. He huddled deeper under the blankets and pulled the covers up around his chin. So he rocked, contorted foetus, rocked and rocked.

The day dawns. I am born. It is like walking out on stage into the spotlight. I do not want to be born. Not here. Not like this. Not in Scotland.

An idea came into his mind. Or maybe it had been there for some time and he hadn't noticed it. It was the idea that Scotland is a state of mind. He had no idea where the idea had come from, or what it meant. Forget it, he thought, but he couldn't.

The more he thought of it, the less sense it made, but at the same time the more he thought of it the more important it sounded, like a nightmarish question in an examination paper: 'Scotland is a state of mind.' Discuss.

He remembered when he was bored as a boy thinking of a word and repeating it over and over again until the word lost its meaning. It became a sound, and a smell and a taste and a texture. Even then he'd go on repeating it, because he knew if he went on long enough the word would draw aside a curtain in his mind and he would see its face.

He tried it with his idea, Scotland is a state of mind, but it didn't work. No moment of revelation came. His idea — but was it his? Hadn't he read it or heard it somewhere? Then who had said it? Hugh MacDiarmid? Kenneth McKellar? John

30

Grogan? It was the kind of thing Grogan might come out with, in his cups.

He reached for the pack of tobacco and and the papers on the floor and rolled himself a slender cigarette. Jinx slunk around the bed and stood facing the wall, her back to him. She looked over her shoulder briefly and licked her lips cynically.

I'll attend to you in a moment, madam.

He lit up and inhaled gingerly. He glanced at the window. Everything was cold and silent out there, as if everybody had died. It was the last day of the year. He had to get up, get out there, sell some holes, pay his rent and buy his bottle. But first he should really make his resolutions.

1) I will save a little money each week and send it to my widowed mother in The Steamies.

2) I will ask Yvonne to give me another chance.

3) I will apologise to Hugh Mitchell for my tasteless behaviour at his party.

4a) I will relinquish my claim to Income Support and seek employment.

4b) I will do whatever work is offered me, be it full-time or part-time, permanent or temporary, however menial, however poorly paid.

4c) If no work is to be had I will be more diligent in my capacity of door-to-door spy-hole salesman until something better comes along.

5) I will relinquish alcohol and scorn the use of tobacco.

6) I will redecorate the shed and receive visitors on Sundays after chapel.

7) I will treat Jinx with the respect deserving of her species.

8) I will refrain from impersonation in any form, except in a professional capacity.

9) I will clear my debt with Mr Semple, my honest landlord.

10) I will polish my shoes more often.

McCoy SHUDDERED AS he cautiously scaled the stairs to his outer door, still feeling fragile. He looked in his dilapidated letter-box to see if an unexpected letter had come his way. One belated Christmas card. From the childlike handwriting on the envelope, he could tell it was from his mother. There was also a letter in a blue envelope. He ripped open this one with shaking fingers and read: Dear Mr McCoy, Please deliver rent arrears to the above address by 5 p.m. today or we will visit you. Yrs truly, G. Semple.

McCoy had to admire the economy of his landlord's way of putting it: We will visit you. As if they were calling round for a cup of tea and a blether.

He rolled the pale blue obscenity into a tight little ball and stuck it in his pocket.

He tugged the Christmas card from its envelope: a rosy cherub bathed in an aura of golden light sat up in an illuminated cradle of straw, watched by beturbaned old men and a donkey with false eyelashes. McCoy was coming up with a caption – 'To be born into this bastarding barnyard . . .' – as he opened the card and uttered a wordless cry of pure joy when he saw the crisp, folded ten-pound note. Love Mum. It would help with the rent.

Things were definitely looking up.

He stuffed the money and the card in his coat pocket and stepped into the mews. He checked that he had his key, that the snib was on the lock, then pulled it shut. The door had a spy-hole, the first he'd put in, for practice, and he had put it in the wrong way, so that people could look in at him as he came to the door, but he couldn't look out at them.

A mistake was a mistake.

As he steadied himself against a wall he caught sight of his reflection in a ground floor window. That hunched, furtive shadow with the shifty eyes was him, what he'd become, a man neither young nor old, dressed in ill-fitting hand-me-downs: the coat courtesy of Oxfam, the jeans from a jumble sale stall. Not to mention the shoes, which were frankly a disgrace. His fleeting image called to his mind old newsreels to do with the plight of refugees. One of those black and white clips with the snow of interference and the inadequate subtitles. In the image of his own face McCoy could make out the shape of an owl-eyed and spectral skull. He skidded away from it, making up a caption to go with the still: An unknown refugee. Then came the voice-over: It is unlikely that he ever reached his destination. Statistically, it is almost certain that he died and was buried in one of the many mass graves on the way to the off-licence.

Dry laughter.

As he walked to an area he'd left unfinished the last time he'd gone out door-to-door, he imagined the area of town he'd already covered as a dark stain spreading over a street-map. In another mood he'd see it differently, think of the canyons of virgin tenement yet to be trod, the thousands of doors crying out to be fitted with spy-holes. In such a mood his brain would reel with the dream of an impossible day in which he sold a hundred holes, giving him a clear profit of two hundred smackers!

The snow was abating as he turned into a street he hadn't covered and hurried into the first close. He stamped the snow from his shoes and brushed it from his coat. It was a good stair. He had never got himself out so early before and this was all to the good. He might catch some lonely breakfasters before they went out. He approached the first door. No spy-hole. There was definitely somebody in: light above the door, a radio playing, kitchen sounds. The name on it was Caroline Sommerville, printed neatly on a piece of card with Letraset.

He rang the bell and braced himself for the sales-pitch – 'Hello, I'm going round the doors fitting spy-holes. It only takes me five minutes and costs three pounds for the Complete Service, parts included!' – but when the door opened the words stuck like a wad of phlegm in his throat. She was young, blonde, nice-looking, and her face shone with health and confidence.

34

'Yes?'

He felt intimidated by her wholesomeness.

'Sorry – I'm going round the doors –' She smiled at him encouragingly. 'I'm fitting these things, for people.' He tugged the flap of his haversack open, brought out one of the spy-holes, and offered it to her apologetically.

She took it between her slender, delicate fingers and examined it carefully, with mild puzzlement, as if she were a guest on *Going For A Song* trying to guess the function and value of an outmoded object of pure frippery. Maybe she was studying Fine Art.

McCoy's formal education had been cut short the day he was expelled from school for smoking marijuana in the playground and lying on top of his first true love, Pauline. Webber, the headmaster, had sent him home with a letter for his parents. Mary McCoy's reaction to her son's expulsion from school had been to cry, then to make him weed the garden and cut the grass. His father had made him take on a job as a labourer in the carpet factory. He had gone on to educate himself after a fashion, with the help of a couple of night classes, and the many books he had borrowed over the years from MacRae and Grogan. Still there persisted in him the resentment of those who feel they have not been given a fair chance in life and are probably right.

'What on earth is it?'

He couldn't resist a touch of the Arthur Negus wisdom as he replied: 'A spy-'ole. Late twentieth century. Scottish.'

His humour provoked only the swift, dismissive smile of her intolerable tolerance of him.

'What does it *do*?'

'It means you can look out, through your door, I mean, when somebody rings your bell, so you can see who's there,' McCoy explained doggedly. There was nothing worse than not getting the laugh when you needed it.

'I *see*. How awfully clever.' She peered at the curiosity between her fingers as if she could not quite believe that it could exist, far less that someone could be showing her such a thing at her door, then bared her young white teeth in a hostile smile.

McCoy snapped into the sales-pitch: 'It costs only three pounds for the Complete Service, parts included!'

She covered her mouth with a hand to stifle a small cough, looked at him with amusement and pity and held out the thing between her fingers. He got the feeling that she would wash her hands after touching it.

'No thank you.'

'It only takes a couple of minutes –' McCoy persisted, and he saw the pity in her eyes harden to a cool irritation.

'No.'

The door was quietly but decisively closed.

Having been pitied, McCoy became pitiful. He did not try his luck at any other doors in the close. The remaining doorways in the street were fitted with speak-entry systems. That did not always put him off hustling holes to complete strangers who did not want them, since they already had a speak-entry system in operation to keep out riff-raff, but it did this morning. He slouched past those neat rows of names and buzzers, scowling at each in turn, scarcely able to credit the times he'd pleaded into those hateful, perforated mouthpieces to be let in to the close to offer his service to the close-dwellers.

To hell with that for a game.

He turned the corner into the next street. Every close he passed had the speak-entry system, the curse of the humble spy-hole salesman working to maintain his dying trade. One of the doors he came to was open, so he ducked into it, stamped the snow from his shoes and sat down. He took out his tobacco and rolled a cigarette, very slowly because of the numbness of his fingers. He smoked it and considered his position. It was a good stair, it had been entirely renovated and redecorated, therefore the tenants might not be dead against the idea of improvements to their property. On the other hand, few of the tenants would be fearful enough – the word to use to them would be prudent – to feel the need for a spy-hole as well as an electronic security device.

But you can't always tell by someone's voice, sir. Many confidence tricksters are expert mimics. Take the present Secretary of State for Scotland, sir. If he can fool people, sir, think how much easier it would be for a practised criminal to delude you over a tin tannoy. If you would bear with me for a moment, sir, I will demonstrate to you how easy it is to impersonate, for instance, a man who reads the gas meter, or to take another example, a police officer. I don't know how you feel about the Poll Tax, sir, but with this revolutionary, new, scientifically tested breakthrough in personalised surveillance equipment, there is no need to pretend that you are not the responsible person of the household when the Poll Tax Protection Squad calls. Never trust a voice, sir, especially when that voice claims to represent the government, for it may turn out to be genuine. No sir, invest in the additional security of this optical device, now available at an unbeatable price and fitted within a few minutes. After all, sir, my very presence at your door is testimony to the fact that the speak-entry system is not infallible.

It was a variation on the I-could-have-been-anyone line he had sometimes used in a desperate attempt to clinch a sale.

A door banged shut somewhere in the close and he heard someone running downstairs. McCoy got to his feet and left the close. It had stopped snowing.

He turned the next corner and saw a couple of kids making a snowman in their small front garden. A few others were throwing snowballs at each other. Their excited cries haunted McCoy's hungover brain long after he had passed them by and turned into another street. Children. Something from the row with Yvonne the night before last began to emerge: she had said something about wanting or not wanting – he couldn't remember which – to have a child.

And she had told him she was late. Oh Christ. A child. It was possible. With Yvonne. She had mentioned it before. She had been mentioning it more often lately. A vague nativity, half labour-ward and half Christmas card, began to paint itself in his mind. The keen sentimentality of his longing made him forget what he was doing and he meandered aimlessly from street to street, scarcely aware of where he was or where he was going.

As he steered himself around a corner, he was forced to skid to a halt, throwing his arms out to keep his balance. There at his feet, groping around in the snow, was an old man on his hands and knees.

'Are you okay?' McCoy asked him. The question was rhetorical: the old man wasn't enjoying himself down there. His predicament was plainly a source of extreme personal torment, yet McCoy couldn't act, couldn't reach down to give him a hand up. He just kept looking at the old man, as if wondering what he was. He looked like such a strange creature, a rare kind of tortoise in his baggy brown raincoat, his face and his hands a mottled purplish colour because of the cold. His little bald head swung from side to side as he tried to move forward.

The old man was crying for help, but it was a quiet, preoccupied 'Help!' – as if he'd long ago given up all hope of a passer-by.

McCoy forced himself to bend down and hook him under both arms. He tried to hoist him to his feet but the old man fell against him and they tumbled in the snow. The old man started thrashing around wildly, digging his sharp little knee into McCoy's gut and dunting his chest with an elbow. McCoy struggled to hold the old man's arms by his sides as he leaned over to retch into the snow. The old fool started shouting for the polis.

Those bony fists dug deep into McCoy's ribs and every so often one of them found its way to his chin. The old fool thought he was being mugged. McCoy had a mind to mug him, because he didn't like him and he needed the money.

'Stop it!' he bawled in the old man's ear, but he went on lashing out and shouting for the polis. As they rolled around in the snow, cursing and shouting for help, McCoy caught the dead breath of the old man's decaying innards and saw that his eyes reeled crazily in his head.

'Are you blind?' he shouted, then felt a fierce pain low in his gut as the old man jabbed his knee in there. He retched again as the blind old featherweight began to belabour him about the head with both fists. McCoy watched, as if under a spell, as his own blood polka-dotted the snow, dimly aware of a voice somewhere far above him. The voice was a woman's voice and it was threatening to call the police. He could still feel the old man's fists doing their stuff on his ribs – he'd obviously been a boxer in his youth – but he was far away from what was happening. Part of him felt impatient that his time was being wasted – it was urgent that he sell some holes – but another part of him wanted to go on lying there in the snow, staring at his own blood, grateful for such a colourful diversion. He looked up and caught sight of a woman leaning out of a second-floor window. She was wearing a frilly nightdress of some kind – either that or it was her kitchen curtains. She held out a meaty arm, wagged her finger at him and shouted:

'You leave that poor auld man alane! Ah've called the polis on ye! Should be ashamed o yersel, beatin up a blind man!'

McCoy put his guard up against a swift right jab, ducked away from the following left and raised his bloodied fingers to the woman at the window.

'Look at that!' he shouted, his voice rich with the injustice of it. 'That's what he did to me!'

'Serves ye right, ya young thug ye!'

'Mind yer own business!' He gave her the v-sign as she slammed her window shut. The old man was now up on his knees, swinging wildly with his fists and uttering a ceaseless tirade of threats and curses. McCoy crawled backwards away from him but couldn't take his eyes off him. He'd become a spectacle of considerable interest: there he kneeled, his guard up in front of his dead eyes, his narrow, bald little skull dodging around as if to evade a sequence of punches from an opponent, jabbing at mid-air with his fists and muttering incoherently:

'Mawnen, cunt ye, mawn! Ah'm ready for ye! Ah'll show ye! Mess wi me, bastarn deed ya cunt ye! Mawn!'

McCoy had to crawl back towards him to retrieve his haversack. The old man's rage had transformed him from a pitiful and infirm victim to a dangerous lunatic.

Two cops came around the corner and broke into a run as soon as they saw him. McCoy did the same, in the other direction, but gave up out of exhaustion before reaching the end of the street. He leaned against a tenement wall and tried to regain his breath till one of them panted level with him. He was red-haired, overweight and on the short side for a cop. He was too out of breath to speak, so that there was a wordless pause as they eyed each other and gulped down the raw December air, exhaling wide plumes of steam from their heaving lungs.

'Name o God,' the cop gasped. 'What's the idea, eh? Training for the marathon?'

McCoy shook his head and indicated that he was still too out of breath to speak. The cop removed his hat and dabbed his brow with a hanky. He put the hat back on, tugging the peak down over his eyes so that he had to tilt his head back a little in order to see.

'You want to give up the fags, pal.'

McCoy nodded, grateful for this morsel of human advice from an officer of the law, for he didn't much like the look of the man's sideburns, which were long, narrow and carefully trained to slant diagonally across his ruddy cheeks and come to fiery points on either side of his tight little mouth.

'Right. The bag.'

McCoy handed him his haversack and began, 'I can explain everything –'

'Save it.'

The cop gripped his arm and led him back along the street to the scene of the crime. And indeed it had developed into quite a scene. The other cop – a tall, dark, morose looking fellow with a walrus moustache – was taking dictation from the woman from the second floor. She had donned a fur-collared coat to come out into the street. She smoked and gesticulated as she talked, wagging the two fingers holding the cigarette as if beating time to a tune. She was clearly dominating the interview completely.

'That's him!' she cried as they approached, her puffed and sallow face animated by two beady, scandalised eyes. 'That's the one! Ah saw him wi my own eyes!'

'Look, let me explain –'

'Aye, that's him awright!' exclaimed the blind man. 'Tell by his voice!'

'One at a time, one at a time!' said the cop taking notes, but the blind man went on interrupting the woman's story to corroborate its details and to underline its pathos by groaning and holding his ribs.

'I was trying to help him up! I came round the corner and there he was, down on his hands and knees in the snow!'

'Ah fell!' the old man whined, 'Ah lost ma stick.'

'One at a time!'

'So I tried to help him to his feet, but he slipped –'

'A likely story! Ah saw ye! Ye were haudin the auld man doon!'

'Haudin me doon!' echoed the old man.

'He thought I was trying to mug him, so he lashed out at me!'

'That's a good yin!'

The morose cop looked at his chubby colleague and rolled his eyes. The chubby one took over:

'Right, first things first. Are you hurt?' he asked the old man.

40

'Of course he's hurt!' cried the woman.

'He's not – it's me who's hurt!' said McCoy. The cop with the sideburns turned to him and told him in an undertone that he would be if he didn't keep his mouth shut.

The morose one took over:

'Any cuts? Bruises?'

The old man looked hurt all over and began to finger his body gingerly as if he were a mass of livid weals.

McCoy was vaguely aware of the faces at the windows. He thought he heard someone shout 'Lock him up!' and someone else adding, 'Throw away the key!'

He showed the cops the bloodstains on his face and hands. The morose one smirked and he could tell the other one was restraining his mirth as he said to the old man:

'Anything stolen?'

The old man fingered his pockets and the chubby cop began to rummage in McCoy's haversack.

'Ma stick, ma white stick!' said the old man.

The cops looked at McCoy and he shrugged.

'I've not got his stick. I was trying to help him up –'

'What's this for?' said the chubby cop, holding up McCoy's hand-drill. The woman looked at it as if it were a weapon.

'It's a hand-drill,' said McCoy.

'A comedian, eh? Ah know it's a drill. Ah asked you what it was for?'

'Drilling holes,' said McCoy.

Sideburns brought his face close to McCoy's and said: 'Are you takin a rise out of me, friend?'

McCoy said that he wasn't.

The two cops now separated, Sideburns leading McCoy away from his colleague and the old man and the woman in the headscarf to a spot a few yards along the road. He took out his notebook.

'Name?'

'McCoy.'

McCoy could almost see the cog turning in the man's brain.

'The real McCoy, eh?'

McCoy closed his eyes and sighed emphatically.

'What's the matter – nae sense o humour? Address?'

'Care of Semple . . .'

41

The cop stopped writing when he heard the address, closed his notebook and put it in his pocket. He pulled out a blue handkerchief, blew his nose noisily and said confidentially: 'So. You're staying at George Semple's?'

McCoy attempted to lessen the lie: 'It's just temporary. He's my landlord –'

The cop nodded and told McCoy to stay where he was. He walked over to his colleague and had a quiet word with him. Both cops talked to the old man now, leaving the woman out of it. She hovered at her closemouth, trying to hear what was being said, until one of them waved her away. Then the old man was sent on his way and Sideburns walked back over to McCoy.

'Get yourself a trader's licence,' was all he said as he handed him the haversack and dismissed him with a nod.

McCoy had sometimes suspected that Semple was somebody in the Masons. He had a furniture warehouse in Leith, owned a number of other properties and usually went round flanked by a couple of guys who could carry pianos on their backs.

We will visit you.

HE GAVE THE tenements a quick once-over as he made his way through the snow. None looked promising so he kept on going, sticking his nose into the odd closemouth to taste the air in there and so assess the situation. The situation was getting worse: from one close came the acid reek of stale cat's piss, from the next a heavy smell – like decomposing turnips except worse. All the walls were pitted and scarred with gang-slogans. The few closes with numbers had them chalked or scored on the stone. Most were doorless and anonymous but for the graffiti. He paused at one and considered going in. It was dark in there and it stank of bad luck, a commodity he was not short of.

He went in anyway.

All the way up those stairs. Like certain postmen McCoy preferred to start at the top and work his way down. Climbing from humiliation to humiliation would have felt somehow worse. At the top he rested for a minute then chapped the first door. No bell. No name. A hollow sound. The tenants had fled. He moved on to the next. A buzzer. A dog barked murderously and he moved on to the next.

A woman in a greyish dressing gown came to the door and looked at him as if he was the latest in a series of her life's disappointments. She looked exhausted to the point of imminent collapse: she leaned against the door-frame, her lank brown hair falling over her eyes. She didn't bother to hold her dressing-gown shut, so that it swung open to reveal her crushed nightdress, beneath which her flesh rolled and sagged. He didn't have the heart to give her the sales pitch. Instead he took out one of the spy-holes and handed it to her, feeling the heat of her

bedwarmed hand and catching the smell – her, or the house?
– and stammered: 'It's the very thing for preventing a
robbery.'

'Robbery?' She shrugged heavily and, with a listless nod of her
head towards the interior of the house, said, 'Nuthin in there
worth robbin, son.'

'Or just if you want to see who's at your door.' McCoy
persisted, 'This is the very thing –'

The woman looked again at the spy-hole in her palm.

'What is it?' she asked.

'A spy-hole.'

'Aw.' She grunted at the thing in her hand scornfully, said
that she didn't need one and pointed to the letterbox. The point
about the letterbox was that it didn't exist. There was just a long
rectangular hole in the door where there had once been a letterbox
but where now there was none.

McCoy shook his head.

'Sorry. I didn't notice that,' he said, cheerfully. A man's voice
shouted somewhere inside the house and she handed back the
hole and slammed the door.

He went down to the next landing. None of the doors had
spy-holes, but none looked as if they could afford to have. He
hurried back downstairs. As he reached the first floor landing a
long needle of light stabbed him between the eyes.

'Is that you, son?'

It was a defenceless old woman. McCoy noted that the door had
a chain but no spy-hole. He was in with a chance.

He hopped from foot to foot and blew into his hands as he
waited for her to unchain the door. The name on it was Bernard.
It was bitter cold and she was taking ages. He could hear her
muttering away to herself and the sound of her voice made him
shudder – the years had honed it to a shrill whine, clean of
all optimism. The door opened a little wider and he made out
her humped and stunted figure against the glaring light in her
hall.

He couldn't get a word in edgeways. She was browned off, she
was saying. Hadnae been over the door, hadnae been able. What
with her arthritis and her rheumatics playing up as well. Hadnae
been round to the shop to get her *People's Friend*. If it wasnae too
much trouble, she wondered, would he mind?

She thought he was somebody, somebody else, somebody not himself. 'No, no, I'll go,' he said, angrily. He had a good mind to Raskolnikov her there and then.

Demonic laughter.

She swung the door open and he stepped in. He waited while she scuffed off to the living-room for her purse. He shut his eyes and shuddered. Oh Christ, wasn't that a terrible sound, that slow scuffing of her slippers on the linoleum? She scuffed back out with a few coins in her claw-like hand.

'And did ye have a guid Christmas, Aleck?'

So he was Aleck. McCoy had never before been asked to impersonate somebody he knew nothing about.

'Aye,' he said, in an Alecky voice.

The old woman looked at him and her eyes rounded in fright.

'Here, you're no Aleck!'

'I know I'm no Aleck,' he said, unable to withhold an echo of the old woman's whiny voice from his own, 'I'm going round the doors selling spy-holes . . .'

The hand that had flown up to her chest began to sag as she listened to his story. He laid it on thick about the danger of not having one, and he was ready for her objection that she already had a chain:

'Oh no, Mrs Bernard, you want to see who you're opening the door to, chain or no chain. Look.'

He demonstrated how a man's arm could easily get through the door even with the chain on.

'After all, Mrs Bernard,' he said grimly, 'I could've been anyone.'

'Thank God you're no,' she said.

He waited impatiently while she considered the matter gravely, then she asked again about the price. She started to hum and haw, so he threw in a concession for O.A.P.s. At last, she agreed. She stood with her arms folded, watching him bore the hole in her door and fit the spy-hole, making sure he didn't skimp his labour on the job.

She paid him and gave him the exact money for her message: two ounces of spam and the *People's Friend*.

'Where's the shop?' asked McCoy.

'Ye'll have tae go tae Laird's, son, up by Gilmore Place –'

45

'Gilmore Place – that's miles away. Is there not somewhere nearer?'

'Aye but my *People's Friend*'s on order frae Laird's, son, and his spam's a better quality than these local shops have. Is it too much trouble?'

'No, no,' muttered McCoy, barely able to contain his impatience, 'I'll go, but it'll take me a while.'

'That's okay son, Ah'm no in any hurry. Ah'll no be gaan anywhere.'

No in any hurry. No be gaan anywhere. The futility of her situation came home to him. He had to go and get her message for her, there was no way round it. He hurried down the stairs, pursued by the thin whine of her thanks.

Outside, the rain had come on heavier. It had been a brutal day so far. Now here he was going people's messages for them and the weather had turned against him. He glared at the sky. It spat in his face. Gilmore Place. All the way up to Dundee Street, then over the Union Canal.

He tugged his coat-lapels together, bowed his head and walked. At least it was a break from the hole-selling. As he walked, his strides took on a rhythm, then the rhythm took on a tune, and the tune had words to it. He began to sing under his breath:

Keep right on to the end of the road,
Keep right on to the end,
Though your heart be weary
Still journey on
Till you come to your happy abode,
Though the way be long,
May your heart be strong –
To the end, to the end, of the ROAAAAAAAAAAAAAAAAD.

It was his father singing inside him, from the corner of the living room designated as the stage for those who wished to take it, though some liked to sing from where they sat, like Mrs Payne. It's New Year. Everybody sings.

'Everybody bar yer mither,' wisecracks John McCoy, then eggs her on: 'Mawnen Mary, gi'us a song!' and she tuts and protests like an agitated bird, no she'll no do anything of the sort and anyway it's time to get the sandwiches, whereupon he raises an

46

arm, at the end of which is a hand, in which is held a glass of whisky, and he holds it up there so that it catches the living room lights and the amber turns to molten gold, and as he brings it to his lips his eyes lose sight of it, so that his lips have to guess where the rim of the glass is, then he upturns it with a quick flick of the wrist and drinks and lets the whisky sing, O Danny Boy, the pipes the pipes are calling, and the shouts for order, order usher a hush into the room so that for a moment John McCoy's slurred, veering voice – a strangely wavering tenor with sudden squirms of alto and plunges into bass – must swell unnaturally to fill the space of the smoke-hung silence of the listening room as he sings and goes on singing, O Danny boy, till his voice is joined by another voice, and another and another and another, until the whole room is singing, From glen to glen . . .

After the song, Jimmy McGeechan, the horned one to the boy McCoy, tells a joke and everybody refills their glasses. The boy McCoy is sitting under the table holding a tiny, gold-rimmed glass adorned with a simple green shamrock. He sniffs the contents, sips, winces and splutters, then feels the whisky numb the tip of his tongue and his gums.

He looks up, sensing a change in the room: Jimmy McGeechan has stopped telling the joke and his father's voice is loud and dangerous as he speaks:

'You owe everybody in this room an apology. Right now.'

'He didnae mean anythin, John,' says his mother. 'Say you're sorry.'

'What did Ah susususus---------ay?'

'Leave him alane, John.'

'Apologise for your language or get out.'

'What la---------nguage?'

'He didnae swear, John,' puts in Mrs Payne wheezily.

'Oh?' says John McCoy, with a threatening rise in his voice, 'In this house, the word scrubber is a swearword!'

'Aw, Johnny, it's no that bad –' says Mrs Payne.

Mrs Schmidt leans over to her husband and begins to ask him in a whisper what scrubber means but he silences her with a dark, German look.

'Ah'm sosososorry,' says Jimmy McGeechan, holding both his hands up in a gesture of surrender. 'Ah didnae mumumumume--------an anythin – it wis just a jojojojo---------ke!'

47

'It's no fuckin joke!' spits his father, and the hush in the room makes everything stand still for a moment.

'That's enough now, John –' says his mother.

'No it's no enough. Who does he think he's talkin aboot, eh? Ye're talkin aboot yersel, ya ignoramus – scrubber, by Christ, and what d'ye think she does for a livin, eh?' He points to Mary and glares at McGeechan, who is now hiding behind his cigarette smoke and looking around the room for support and protection.

'Aw c'mon now, be re---------asonable John, it wis just a joke, Ah didnae mean Mamamama---------ry, when you call somebody a "scrubber", ye mean –'

'Ah know what the word means!' His father's colour mounts as his voice pounds the air: 'It's yer own class you're talkin aboot, ya ignorant swine! Say you're sorry!'

'Ah'm *sososososo*---------*rry*!'

McCoy sees his mother adjust her glasses as she starts to cry. He runs over the room to her, but throws his words at his father:

'Daddy, can Ah tell a joke?'

'Aye, good idea, let the bairn tell us a joke, cheer us up!' says Mrs Payne, clapping her meaty hands.

The Schmidts nod stiffly in approval.

And so the boy McCoy brings peace to the room, taking the stage, while his father goes over to McGeechan, who has retreated to the sideboard to refill his tumbler, and McCoy can see his father's hand patting his friend's shoulder as both men make friends again in private. The boy McCoy has done this before, and already he knows to wait for the attention of the room before he begins:

'This big shark is swimmin through the sea an he sees a wee octopus . . . naw, a squid. So he says tae hissel: the very thing fur ma breakfast. But the squid hauds up his tentacles an says, Aw naw, dinnae eat me, Ah'm no feelin weel. Ah've got the cauld an Ah dinnae taste very nice . . . So the shark says, Is that right, awright well, Ah'll just keep ye till ye get better, then Ah'll eat ye! So the shark tucks the squid under his fin an away he swims through the sea, till he meets anither shark – his pal Bill. So he says, Haw Bill, how's it gawn? Oh, by the way, there's that sick squid Ah owe ye!'

As the room erupts, McCoy runs through the laughter and the applause to his mother, who has dried her eyes and is smiling . . .

'Gi'us Danny Boy again, John!'

'Aye, one more time!'

'Order, order!'

'One singer one song!'

'O Danny boy, the pipes, the pipes are calling, from glen to glen –'

As he reached the bridge, the break in the tenements made McCoy slow his stride and look out along the Union Canal. Despite the snow, the view was a sombre one: tall tenements on either side of a narrow sluice of greenish water. But it was a view, something with distance in it. He followed the canal with his eye until it curved out of sight. Above the rooftops of the tenements he could see the pale contours of the Pentland Hills.

Across the mountainside –

Laird's turned out to be a licenced grocer's, a traditional establishment which sold cooked meats, wines and spirits, vegetables, tinned goods, jars of jam, newspapers and a great variety of shortbreads, some of which came in tins adorned with panoramic views of the Highlands, others with tartan-tammied terriers.

McCoy took his place in the queue. The shop was busy. He was in no mood for it, nor for its proprietor, who was a gentleman grocer of the old kind, sporting not only a collar and tie beneath his grey nylon shop-coat but also a black waistcoat. McCoy watched him as he bustled about his business, wrapping cold meats in greaseproof paper, giving his assistants their orders, taking his pencil from behind his ear and tallying up the totals on the back of a brown paper bag, having a chat with his customers, clapping his hands together with relish. For a man of over fifty he seemed almost obscenely healthy, his ruddy complexion shining in the shop light, which winked from his gold-rimmed spectacles merrily. His cheeriness was undaunted by the queue of customers waiting to be served; if anything it made him all the more hearty as he sliced another ham, enquiring after the health of the old lady he served and glancing at his watch as she told him that interminable tale of woe.

It fell to McCoy to be served by one of his assistants, a fed-up teenage schoolgirl – the Laird's daughter? – no doubt working here over the Christmas break from school.

'Two ounces of spam, please,' said McCoy.

49

He thought he heard someone titter in the queue behind him. The Laird glared at him coldly as he filled a carrier bag with cake and liqueurs and shortbread.

The young girl glanced at him with her lovely, slovenly, adolescent brown eyes. 'Two ounces?' And the eyes said, Is that all?

'It's for an old lady.'

McCoy doing his best to resemble a guardian of the elderly housebound. Even so, he could tell that this young girl did not believe him. He caught sight of himself in the old mirror advertising whisky behind the counter. He looked rough. He looked untrustworthy.

'Anything else?'

'A ham roll and a corned beef roll.'

He would need something to eat later on.

She sighed heavily as she turned to make up his rolls, which she did with patent reluctance, so much so that her father – McCoy now felt sure that she must be his daughter – told her to get a move on.

'There are other customers!' he said to her in a hurried whisper.

'Fancy – Spam at New Year!' whispered someone in the queue behind him. McCoy affected nonchalance and something of the air of the eccentric millionaire as he turned to survey the other customers.

'There is nothing wrong with Spam, no matter what time of the year it is!' he announced, and the shop fell silent. 'It may not be a festive meal, although perhaps a sprig of holly . . .'

There was a stunned pause before the old ladies in the queue realised that a joke had been made and started wheezing and cackling with laughter.

The Laird eyed McCoy with a new interest and called over his shoulder to his daughter: 'Give the poor boy an extra slice!' The young girl looked over at him and smiled lazily. McCoy eyed her legs with a hunger as urgent as it was hopeless. A grocer's daughter. That was what he needed. If he played his cards right he could inherit the business and the grey shop-coat: McCoy's Licensed Grocery. Fine Victuals, wines and spirits. He could see it. His routines would be put to good use at last. A captive audience at last.

Her legs were all right, but McCoy knew his lust was misplaced
– it had been a long time, the best part of a month, since he
had slept with Yvonne, and the last time it hadn't been up to
much. After a dull night in the pub with the Out-crowd, he had
persuaded her to drift into a drowsy submission, but she had
been out to lunch and, if the truth be told, in his case there had
been nobody at home either. Surely all that worked against the
possibility of conception, sub-standard condom or not.

Let her not be. Not this time. Not like this. I need more time.
I need more space. I need more money –

'Anything else?'

Her pouting, adolescent resentment had now returned and it
only served to aggravate McCoy's need to scratch that old itch
that burned to be scratched again. It was the last day of the year.
He must see it out with a bang.

'The *People's Friend*.'

'Is it ordered?'

'Yes. The name's Mrs Bernard.'

The girl dragged her feet over to the counter with the papers
and fished out one from a pile.

He felt the clammy palm of her hand touch his fingertips as he
paid.

On the way out of the shop, he paused outside the door to
glance at the various handwritten cards in the window. One card
in particular caught his eye:

SHOES FOR SALE
ONE PAIR (GENTS) OXFORD BROGUES (UNWORN)
SIZE 8 – NOT IMPERFECT – TEN POUNDS (o.n.o.)

McCoy fished a biro from his haversack, the Christmas card
from his mother, and took a note of the name and address, which
was in Tarvit Street. Size eight might be a bit on the tight side,
but a pair of brogues would certainly do the trick as far as hoofing
it round the doors went. Especially in weather like this. The pair
he was wearing were letting in, the situation was an emergency.
Anyway he hated them.

And he eyed his shoes with hatred as he retraced his steps to
Mrs Bernard's door. He had bought them at the January sales
last year, after he'd dragged himself from one end of Princes

51

Street to the other, trying on all kinds of two-tone efforts and slip-on monstrosities. There had been the difficulty of trying to find a pair which could be worn on stage as well as for everyday use. He had never grown to like the pair he had ended up with, the pair he was now wearing. The colour had always been wrong. Light tan, now stained and cracked and sad.

A pair of Oxford Brogues. Unworn. Not imperfect.

The pinpoint of light in Mrs Bernard's door was eclipsed as her eye came to it.

'Is that you, son?'

'Aye, it's me,' said McCoy, sounding more like Aleck than ever.

She went through the long and laborious business of unlocking her door.

'You werenae long, son. Ah've put the kettle on –'

Though he was as dry as a bone he refused her offer of a cup of tea, gave her her message and ran back down the stairs.

He had to get out of here, had to find a better area. This one was too much like home. He had to find the right kind of street – not too rich, not too poor – but when he came to the end of one street and saw that the next was no different, something made him keep on going rather than turn back.

Sometimes he wished he could clang a bell as he went through the streets, crying his wares – 'Spy-holes, spy-holes! Come and get your spy-holes!' – as people were supposed to have done in the old days. Not so long ago that McCoy could not remember one or two of them himself – and what were they, if not his predecessors: the knife-sharpener; the rag-and-bone man; the man from the Prudential; the toffee apple man.

An old fear stirred inside him, inside him where his mother was telling him to come away from the window, not to heed that garbled cry like a broken yodel that had drawn him there, telling him the toffee apple man was an old rogue, that he poisoned the toffee apples to make the children ill, but still he stands at the window, glued there by his mingled greed for the toffee apple and his fear of the dark, mufflered, bunnetted figure of the toffee apple man under the streetlamp, the breath steaming from his mouth like some infernal smoke in the cold night air, as he cries his wares throughout The Steamies. An old fear, but now it took on a new shape: that he was becoming the toffee apple man

52

himself, poisoning people's minds with his diabolical spy-holes and threatening innuendoes.

He let the haversack slip from his shoulder, caught it by the strap and began to swing it around his head.

'Spy-'oles! Spy-'oles! Come an get ya spy-'oles!'

A man getting into a van on the other side of the street looked at him as if he was mad.

HER BREATH STEAMED, she felt the cold nipping her eyelids and she could hear the soft creaking noise of the snow being compressed under her feet as she walked along by the water of Leith, sometimes stopping to look over the fence at the frozen river.

She had put on the black dress – not for its nostalgia value, not to go into mourning either, but just because it happened to be the one she'd taken from the rail. It wasn't warm enough for the weather. She resented the way the cold was making her nipples stand to attention, the more so because in this was contained a memory of the first time they'd met. At the club in Denny, with her dad. Not only had she been wearing the same dress, but her nipples had done the same when she'd seen him sitting down across from her after coming offstage and she'd felt the same resentment about it.

She wouldn't have spoken to him if he hadn't knocked over her glass. It was a stupid way to meet. But she had seen something in him that needed her. He had made her feel attractive.

Before coming out, she had looked at herself in the mirror and wondered if she was still attractive. And as soon as the question had come into her mind, she knew that she was, and as soon as she knew that she was still attractive, it occurred to her that she didn't care, that it made no difference to her if she was attractive or not. Then she wondered if her indifference to her own attractiveness would make her more or less attractive to others.

' There were times when she felt attractive in herself and at these times she seemed to become attractive to others: men or women, children or pensioners, all seemed to realise unanimously that she was there and that she was uniquely herself – and as such, uniquely attractive. In such a mood, she would be disconcerted

54

to find that some of her fifth-year boys were giving her meaningful looks. The male teachers were no more subtle, and could be so crass in their overtures that it was always difficult to say with any certainty that they were being really serious and have them by the balls for harassment.

He didn't understand what it was like. He didn't know what it meant to have to go out there every morning, in that car with the others, and stand there in front of thirty pairs of eyes and perform, perform as yourself, nobody else. She knew that was what you had to do, but equally well she knew that she wasn't all that good at it, and that almost always she ended having to be someone else, someone not herself. That was what was so awful about it, hearing your own voice sounding like someone else's. Shut *up*! Keep *still*! Eyes on the *blackboard*!

On the blackboard of her recent nightmares there is nothing but dust. When she tries to erase it with the duster, she is enveloped by a cloud of chalk dust, so fine it floats in the air, gets in her hair, under her nails, settles on her lipstick as she breathes it in, until she begins to choke. She would wake up from such dreams gasping for breath and full of nameless forebodings about going in to face the third year. Once or twice she had called in sick, and it wasn't so far from the truth. The chalk dust was making her sick, she was sure of it, breathing it in from day to day, from year to year. It would fill her up, until her insides were encrusted with it, encasing every nerve, cauterising every brain-cell, until one day someone or something would pluck the last of the flesh from the exoskeleton and there she would be, the fully calcified teacher.

And there were all the other awful things about it – the exam futility, the staff-room intrigue, the petty disputes about supplies. Cuthbert, the head of department, had been getting to her lately. On top of the way he was failing to run the department, he'd become obsessive about paper. He hoarded it all in his store-room, along with the sets of texts that had withstood the ravages of time in more senses than one. They were disgusting. She had been supporting him all through his wife walking out on him, and now he was back on the booze. She was running the fucking department for him, carrying the bastard on her back, all right, she chose to do that, she was the A.P.T. and it was her job to do what he couldn't. But the paper thing was the end. Without paper, what could you do?

The school was running down, every day it was getting worse, everyone wanted out. Every Thursday it was a dogfight between Cathy Lyon and Helen Aitken to get to the *T.E.S.* first to scan the Situations Vacant. Hugh Mitchell had done it. He was leaving. He was escaping to Islay where the career prospects wouldn't be up to much but the teaching would be fine, the lifestyle relaxed. It was absolutely the right thing to do, the only thing to do. She could have gone with him. If. He had made more than one pass at her.

She felt guilty about thinking about it, then wondered if it was possible to be unfaithful to somebody who's dead. It would make it more difficult, that's all. But that was nothing to do with it, faithful or unfaithful wasn't the issue. Maybe she was feeling guilty because she knew that she was going through one of those times when she was attractive to other people, one of those times when even babies looked at her with more intent than they should have.

Babies. They'd been getting to her since Christmas, which she'd spent at her younger sister Jacky's house in Falkirk, having shots of holding her two-month-old niece. Now she couldn't seem to get away from the cooing, gurgling, crying, sicking, sucking things. They were everywhere. You couldn't switch on the t.v. without seeing one crawling round in a nappy it didn't know it was advertising. And now, walking along the water of Leith and trying to keep his death in her mind, she kept passing mothers and fathers pushing buggies and prams and all she could think of was babies. She wasn't sentimental about the idea of having her own. She knew exactly what it would involve, the hours it would take up with the changing nappies and the making up bottles and the exhaustion from the lack of sleep. She had the kind of imagination which dealt in such practicalities and had a fair idea of the daily drain on her energies a baby would be. But now she wondered if not having a father around would necessarily simplify things.

She stopped to look over the railings, but moved on as soon as she heard people approaching.

She felt exposed, as if she were naked. People seemed to be looking at her oddly, as if they could tell that there was something not right with her.

Another family unit, Mum and Dad and two kids, passed her and despite herself, she felt obliged to nod and smile falsely at them.

The father responded with, 'A good day for it.'

What did that mean? A good day for what – snow? A good day for birth. A good day for death.

When the bridge came into view, she no longer looked at the water or the people passing. The bridge, the very height of it, kept drawing her eye upwards. It reminded her of a striding giant in a book of fairy tales, who had given her nightmares as a girl.

He had jumped. From up there.

She stopped under the bridge and looked around. There was no sign that it had happened. What did she expect – a man-shaped hole in the ice? An area cordoned off by the police? A bloodstain? Something. But there was nothing to show that it had happened. A brief hope rose inside her and it was as if, by an imperceptible rise in its level, the water began to overflow the dam. She cried awkwardly and angrily, with tight, shuddering sobs and hot tears that stung her cheeks.

If only she could wail the way the Greek women wailed, the way they were expected to wail, the way they had been taught to wail. It would be better than this clenched, ugly, wracking agony.

A crow flapped from a high treetop and flew overhead cawing raucously.

HE BOUGHT THE holes from a wholesaler – the pun sometimes amused friends but had long ago gone stale on McCoy – who inhabited a dank premises near Leith docks. He was a laconic, taciturn man with an ugly scar on his cheek. He never spoke to him except to say what was necessary for their small but meaningful business transactions.

The holes worked out at just under a quid each. He charged three pounds for the Complete Service, parts included, which gave him a clear profit of 200 per cent on each sale, but sales were few and far between even on a good day. So many people thought he was trying to convert them to a religion, or to double-glazing, that it was often impossible to get the sales pitch out before the door was shut on him. Even when he did manage to say his little piece, people were usually reluctant to commit themselves there and then, whereupon he would launch into The Patter.

The Patter varied with his mood, the weather, how many holes he'd sold so far and, of course, the customer. Some were much more wary of him than others and it was to these that he laid it on thickest, hoping his overtures wouldn't be wasted. 'After all, I could've been anyone!' was meant to be the clinch-line.

It had clinched the odd sale in the past. He remembered one well-dressed woman smiling at him tensely, as if restraining a scream, before respectfully agreeing to have the spy-hole fitted – if only to forestall opening her door to the likes of McCoy again. More often than not the I-could've-been-anyone line prompted people to look him up and down, conclude that he was anyone and shut the door in haste. Either way it introduced an element of threat he didn't much relish. It was better to come away from a transaction feeling that he'd provided a necessary service at an economical rate, but mostly he didn't come away feeling this. Mostly he came away, sale or no sale, feeling that he'd been appealing to the paranoia people harboured in their hearts, whether the monsters they most feared were the cops or the robbers.

Sometimes he'd disgust himself by including in The Patter a story about a seventy-five-year-old woman in a wheelchair who'd answered her door to a stranger only to be brutally murdered and robbed. This little horror story, which he was always adding to and changing to suit the customer, was based on a report in the *Evening News*. In the original the woman had been in her fifties, no cripple and hadn't been assaulted at all. She'd just been robbed of a few pounds by a man who had gained access by claiming he'd been sent round by the Council to test for subsidence.

McCoy had come a long way from his source, sometimes making his pensioner blind as well as lame. Once, he'd inflicted a rare blood disease on her, only to find out that the woman at the door had it and was anxious to contact a fellow-sufferer. And sometimes he'd elaborate lurid details of the crime, like the length of lead-filled hose with which the psychotic killer had dispatched his victim. The final injustice was of course the insanity verdict returned by the jury.

But although he felt disgusted with himself, his disgust didn't stop him embroidering the story a little more each time he told it, and sometimes he'd come away feeling strangely elated about his latest outlandish departure from the truth, as if his version had outstripped the paper's and had come into its own. The strange thing was that the more unlikely he made the story, the more convincing it seemed to become. In many eyes he'd read the belief that outside the door mayhem ruled, the only trouble being that this usually made the potential customer desperate to shut and bolt the door on him, the bringer of bad tidings. Stranger still – he himself had started to believe in the story he told them, with guess-who in the role of psychopath.

When he wasn't appealing to the paranoia of others, he was feeling it himself, convinced that the next door would be opened by a desk-clerk from the D.H.S.S. with a photographic memory. In such a mood he was reluctant to launch into The Patter and instead tried to speak to the customer's common sense, often emphasising the utility appeal of the spy-hole by taking the hand-drill out of his haversack and displaying it. If the customer went on humming and hawing, he'd hand him one of the spy-holes and invite him to look through its tiny, fish-eye lens. As long as it was in the customer's hand he knew that he could go on talking about how quick and useful the service he was offering really was. Even when a customer tried to hand it back to him, McCoy could pretend not to notice and give them the Patter. He remembered a man who had agreed to have it fitted out of exasperation, so that he could get back to his tea. Another time a woman putting her curlers in had ended their interview by dropping the spy-hole at his feet and slamming the door.

As he tramped through the snow – it was fast turning to slush – he thought bitterly of the young woman who'd scuppered him before he'd got started by being unable to conceal her pity for him. Her pity hadn't moved her enough to buy a hole, so what good was it to him? It didn't keep the heavies from his door. It didn't stop Semple putting his stuff out into the street.

Better if she'd laughed in his face and told him where to stick his spy-hole! If she'd been old and ugly, a different story then no doubt, but she'd been young, good-looking and he'd fancied her strongly, the bitch.

Christ, he could throw in the towel right now and get a bus – no, a taxi – to the New Town, where Yvonne would probably be sitting in front of the fire in her comfy little one-bedroom flat, reading a book or listening to tapes or watching a video. There would be a pot of hot coffee. He could throw himself at her mercy.

Christ, Yvonne, I'm really fucking sorry about the night before last. No, really, I mean it. That's all I came to say. I don't expect you to forgive me, I'm not asking to be let in out of the cold, even although it's nearly the New Year, I don't expect you to even want to talk to me. I know things haven't been all that great lately between you and me, and I'm broke and I haven't got a job and I'm not getting anywhere as a comedian, but believe me, Yvonne, I didn't want it to work out like this, I didn't sit down and plan my life to be the way it is –

Mibbe you should've. Then it might've turned out better.

That's what she'd say. Something like that. But then he'd concede the point:

I know, I know, my life's a mess. I should've kept on with the night classes. Actually, I'm thinking of signing up for one or two next month, but it's the money.

No, better to leave money out of it. And education.

Anyway, Yvonne, I just came round to say sorry and wish you a happy New Year when it comes, I mean after all, whatever else happens, I'm still you and you're still me, eh?

Not that line again. It had worked a few times in the past but it was definitely wearing thin, like a joke going stale. He'd have to think of something better to clinch their making up.

How about something like this: You and me, Yvonne, whatever else happens, we're still us, eh?

Or how about: Yvonne, I've thought about it and I've realised you're right. It's time we lived together. Your place, or mine?

That should do it.

Then, with luck, the wishful, wistful New Year kiss would develop into something more feeling and she would invite him in.

If he laid his cards on the table, she would see him the money for the rent he owed, she was good that way. She understood that he had always been reckless with the little money he got his hands on, and though she sometimes villified him for it, she would not have had him otherwise, and had told him so more than once, for though she was never extravagant herself, she despised thrift in others, especially men. But then he knew how it would be. He would feel obliged to be grateful and, after half-an-hour of that, she would feel obliged to resent his obligation to her, and then she would resent the fact that she was being made to feel obliged to be resentful, because she didn't want to be resentful, she wasn't a resentful person . . .

O Lord, please don't let me be misunderstood, deedle-ee deedle-ee, deedle-ee-dee-dee-dee. Life has its problems. Ah got more'n ma share. Dee-deedlee, deedle-ing, deedlee-ee-dee-dee-dee . . .

The Animals from the record player in the corner of the Loanhead Youth Club Dance went on playing their electric guitars inside him as he turned another corner and kept on going, no longer even looking at the tenements as he hurried past them, because he remembered having covered this area a few weeks ago. That was one of the drawbacks of the work:

61

once you'd done it, you couldn't do it again. In that respect window-cleaning beat it hands down.

He turned a corner and, at last, came to a street that looked good. The windows had curtains. One or two window boxes. This was it. This had to be it. 'Excuse me, I'm going round the doors . . .' He swung open the gate of a basement flat and padded down the worn stairs. It didn't look so good after all. Where others might cultivate pot plants, the tenants here had cultivated a mound of dismembered chairs. It looked as if a wardrobe had been recently hacked apart as well. The need for fuel had become urgent apparently. The mound of wood was covered loosely with a polythene sheet, held down by a rusted axe. By the door stood an old enamel bread-bin full of rainwater and litter. On a scrap of torn cardboard sellotaped to the door there was a jumble of names printed in biro. One or two had been scored out and others added and below them there was the legend 'mail for' and another long list of names. It didn't look promising at all.

Nevertheless McCoy rapped purposively on the door, then noticed to his horror that the door already had a spy-hole. It was a more elaborate one than those he was touting, with a wider lens and a brass trim.

McCoy struck his head with his fist and cursed his own stupidity. As he did, he had the feeling that he was being watched. He was right – as he turned to go he heard a faint voice:

'Who are you?'

'No one! It's all right!'

'What do you want?'

'Nothing! It's okay, I'm going!'

But something in the voice held him there. He needed to explain himself. He stood where he'd be clearly seen and explained that he was a spy-hole salesman and hadn't noticed that the door already had one. It sounded unlikely, so he took the hand-drill out of his haversack and held it up.

'Sorry to have bothered you. Have a good New Year! Goodbye!' The door opened a crack and a pale eye probed him from inside. He thought he recognised her from somewhere.

'Hello there – how're you doing?'

'Okay.'

But things didn't look okay. The voice was edged with fear and the eyes had a hunted look. McCoy tried a reassuring smile. The door closed a little. Suddenly he wanted in, wanted one door not to shut him out but admit him, wanted to gain access. What was her name? He ran his eye down the list of names on the door. She saw him do it:

'It's Alison. It's not on the door yet though.'

'Alison, of course! Patrick. We met at a party, eh?'

He thought he saw her nod uncertainly. The door opened a little more and he saw her more clearly. She was small and skinny, with short fairish hair in a Dennis-the-Menace punk-cut. She looked washed-out. Even so, there was a strange intensity about her. Her face had a frail beauty, with delicate cheekbones and lips, but there was something wrong in her big, pale blue eyes. They should have been dreamy, wondering eyes. Instead they looked violated.

'Who've you come to see?'

McCoy hesitated. He could say he'd come to see her, but she'd want to know why, and how he'd found out her address. He thought of picking a name at random from the list on the door – Pete, say – but what if Pete turned out to be in?

'I haven't really come to see anybody. Did you not hear what I said about the spy-holes?'

'Spy-holes?'

She glanced at the one in the door and looked at him suspiciously. He explained himself again – why did the truth, in his mouth, sound so much like a stream of lies? – then asked her if he might use the toilet. She reluctantly agreed. He thanked her and sidled past her into the narrow hallway, made more narrow by the furniture stacked along one wall. The toilet was there just inside the door. She flicked the light switch for him and he went in.

Though his need was genuine he was unable to make a splash, conscious of the girl waiting out there on the other side of the door. He looked around the walls. They were a mess. It looked as if many small pictures had been recently torn down, taking bits of the paint off with them. Scraps of torn newspaper were jammed into the toilet-holder.

Home sweet home.

McCoy shut his eyes and tried to concentrate on the sound of the rain against the window behind him. It made him feel that he was in, that he had gained access, and he smiled with gratitude and longing.

His piss rattled into the pan.

SHE FLUNG THE papers on the coffee table, switched the gas fire on and kicked off her shoes. They shot across the floor and smacked against the skirting board. Seeing a solitary apple in the fruit bowl, she picked it up and took a bite, then dropped it back in the bowl. She tugged her coat off and threw it at the couch, then stamped through to the kitchen to make more coffee.

Her skin tingled from the cold, the rims of her ears were smarting and her fingers had gone numb. She blew into her hands and rubbed them together, then held them against her ears. She began to feel the warmth of the flat surround her, but there was a hard, sharp cold inside her that couldn't be reached, as if an icicle had cut into her and lodged in her flesh. It hurt when she moved. It hurt when she breathed.

She took a mug of coffee back through to the fire, lit a cigarette, sat down and turned over the pages of the newspaper hurriedly. She couldn't see anything about the death. There had been other deaths, but his wasn't there. That was typical. Nothing was straightforward, everything had to be difficult. But maybe it was too soon. Or maybe it had been in yesterday's paper and she'd missed it. No. A death like his would be bound to be reported.

When she had gone through the obituaries and found nothing, she threw the paper on the floor and pulled the phone towards her. She had to phone somebody to confirm it. She pulled the phone book towards her and opened it, wondering what the morgue would be listed under. She could start by phoning round the hospitals, but she wanted to speak to someone, if not his mother then someone else who knew him. Not a friend. Someone who knew him but didn't know her, someone neutral but not mutual. She wanted to hear herself saying it, to be heard by someone else saying it, that would make it real. Someone to do with *The Hogmanay Show*. They should know, they should be informed. They had to be. They would put something on before the programme. An announcement. An announcement would surely make it final. She remembered him talking about the producer called MacDonald or McDonald who lived in Edinburgh. She turned to the name in the phone book. There were hundreds of them. It might take her all day to find the right one.

She phoned STV and was told Mr McDonald wasn't in the building, and that his home phone number couldn't be given out. But she found out that his first name was Donald and that he was a McDonald rather than a MacDonald. That narrowed it down to less than a hundred possible names. It was a course of action, a practical task. She found a pen to cross off the numbers as she tried them, poured herself another mug of coffee and started going through the list.

HE CAME OUT with dripping hands to find that she'd gone inside. He edged along the hallway to find her standing in the doorway of her room – it looked like a box-room.

'You wouldn't have a towel, would you?' said McCoy, inclining his head in the style of a tramp at the door asking for a glass of water.

She pulled one from a hook behind the door and handed it to him. He dried his hands, then asked her if it was okay to do his hair. As she shrugged and said she didn't see why not, he noticed that she was wearing an old dressing-gown and that there were deep, dark marks under her eyes.

'Are you not well?' McCoy the concerned friend.

'What makes you say that?'

'You look a bit pale.' Reaching for his stethoscope.

'I'm anaemic.'

'Oh,' said McCoy, but even this, this non-committal mono-syllable, was not his entirely. It was his mother's vague 'Oh', the one that meant she wasn't really listening to what was being said and wanted to change the subject.

He handed her back the towel and thanked her. Then, he sneezed.

'Maybe it's me who's ill.'

He saw a ripped armchair among the furniture in the hall and said, 'You wouldn't mind if I waited there, would you?' The tramp again, this time asking for a bed.

'Waited?'

'Till the rain goes off. I'm drenched. It's pouring out there!'

She didn't look too happy about it. Her eyes widened as she

stared at the old armchair, as if she didn't quite understand what was being asked of her.

'Just until the rain goes off,' McCoy urged, now moving into the spy-hole salesman in action. No commitments, Madam, and the inconvenience will be minimal.

At length he stood there and looked as pitiful as he could, moving from foot to foot and scratching his head somewhat in the manner of Laurel waiting for Hardy. Having looked pitiful, McCoy was pitied:

'You don't have to wait in the hall. D'you want some tea?'

'I could do with some.'

She told him to wait in the box-room while she went off to make the tea. Apart from one upright chair, a one-bar electric fire and a single bed jammed into a recess in the back wall, the room was bare of furniture. The walls were painted a heavy, sludge-green colour and there was nothing on them – no picture, calendar or mirror. The door had a yale lock on it and a small window which had been painted over with the sludge-green. Lower down there were a few holes drilled in the wood for ventilation.

He draped his coat over the chair-back and squatted on his hunkers and hunched and shuddered in front of the fire. Behind the fire there was a pile of rubble and plaster dust. Looking up, he saw where it had come from: above his head there was a ragged hole in the ceiling.

Alone with himself, McCoy became anxious. He stood up and paced around the room. Though there was no furniture, it felt cramped, airless. He stopped at the bed and leaned over it. From its dishevelled sheets arose the musty odour of something wholesome gone sour. On the floor beside the bed, a jamjar lid had been used as an ashtray and a travelling bag spilled its contents.

He had to get out of here. He had to sell some holes. He had to phone Yvonne and apologise for the night before last and find out if she was or if she wasn't.

He padded along the hall to the rear of the flat. He opened a door, stuck his head in and, seeing the pearly flesh of a woman's breasts and thighs, hastily withdrew it. The woman, kneeling astride a muscular shadow, had looked directly at him but hadn't seemed to see him. McCoy, just outside the door, sneezed again and the woman cried out indignantly.

McCoy caught the man's eye and something happened that had never happened before – except on stage, when he was imitating somebody. The overcoat feeling. He was there, outside the door of the room, but he was there in the bed as well, with the woman, reaching out to shut the door. He had stepped inside the Other again, but this time it wasn't somebody he was impersonating, it was a real person, a complete stranger.

The door was kicked shut and a male voice told him to get lost.

'I'm sorry! I was looking for the kitchen!'

'It's not in here!'

The woman let out a low laugh.

He padded past the door and came to another. The sound of a boiling kettle. He knocked and went in.

'Can I give you a hand?'

'Take these through.'

She handed him a tin tray. Two cracked and stained mugs, a bag of sugar with a soup-spoon sticking out of it, a sagging carton of long-life milk. He waited till she'd filled the tea-pot, stealing a hungry look at her slender neck as she tilted her head and a not-so-hungry look at the frying pan, where a mouse had recently left its tracks in the fat.

Along the hall. The unmistakable sounds of coitus.

She sat on the floor and poured out the tea. She gave him his and took her own, wrapping her hands around the mug and sipping at the tea. She stared at him steadily and McCoy began to fidget.

'What is it you do again, Alison?'

'Why d'you need to know that?'

'I don't. I just wondered.'

He looked around the room for something to talk about, but there was nothing.

'I know what you're thinking. You're wondering why I put the furniture out in the hall, aren't you?'

'No, I can't say I was, but now that you mention it –'

'Now that I mention it, you want to know, is that it?'

'Look, Alison, I don't know what you're getting at, but –'

'What are you getting at?'

'Nothing!'

'That's what they all say.'

'All who?'

'All the others. Every time I ask them what they're getting at they say nothing.'

'Mibbe it's true. Mibbe nobody's getting at anything.'

'You said I was.'

'Did I?'

'Don't play games.'

'Look, Alison, all I meant was –' he tried to remember how the conversation had got off on such a wrong footing. 'All I meant was . . . I wasn't really wondering about the furniture at all, but since you mention it I'm naturally a bit curious, that's all.'

'Curious.'

She repeated the word over and over again between sips of her tea, turning the corners of her mouth downwards, as if either the word or the tea tasted bad.

'If you don't want to tell me,' said McCoy the analyst, restraining the urge to adjust his half-moon spectacles, 'that's understandable.'

'Curious . . .'

He tried to change the subject:

'You haven't been here long, then?'

'How did you find that out?'

'Well, you said you hadn't put your name on the door.'

'There might be other reasons for that.'

'True.'

McCoy gulped his tea and thought about leaving. It was wet out there. It was freezing. It was Edinburgh. It was the last day of the year.

A heavy silence threatened to descend on them which was no silence at all, but rich with the enraptured moans and groans from the room next door. To break it, McCoy enquired:

'So how long have you been here then, Alison?'

'Long enough. Too bloody long.'

'How d'you mean?'

'A fortnight.'

'That isn't so long.'

'Long enough in this place.'

'Don't you like it here?'

'Would you?'

'Well –'

'It's a cave. It's a cupboard. It's worse – look at those air-holes in the door! It's like an animal hutch, for Christ's sake!'

She hunched her shoulders and stared at the door with fierce, frightened eyes.

'Oh, I don't know . . .' said McCoy, searching the room for something good to say about it, 'It's quite . . . cosy, in a way.'

'Cosy.'

'At least it's warm.'

'Cosy.'

'I mean, if you think this is bad, you should see –'

'Cosy.'

'I live in a shed. I'm the only person I know with an outside kitchen. It's infested with rats. Jinx, my cat –'

'Cosy.'

'Well, not cosy then, but . . . Maybe if you painted the walls –'

'I just have.'

'Oh.'

A moment of toil for McCoy. Why did everything have to feel like work?

'I suppose that's why you moved the furniture out, eh?'

'No. That isn't the reason at all.'

'Forget it. I don't want to know.'

The mention of the furniture seemed to agitate her. Her eyes darted from side to side as if she was listening to something, some voice only she could hear.

'It's a good colour, that green.' He leaned back in the chair to assess the green wall more professionally.

'You don't like it, do you?' said Alison, looking at the floor.

'As a colour it's rich, and it's good and solid, it's mibbe just a shade too dark, that's all.'

'I know it's dark. It's meant to be.'

'I can see that. I just meant it's a bit on the dark side, for a box-room, I mean.'

'It's a cave. I didn't see much point in trying to make it look light and airy.'

'I see what you mean. All the same, a picture or two on that wall wouldn't go wrong.'

He was startled to notice the look of intense distrust in her eyes.

71

'What's the matter, Alison?'

She said nothing, but went on staring at him with alarmed eyes, her face a taut mask of anxiety. He made to place a reassuring hand on her shoulder, but she recoiled, holding her arm up in front of her face as if to fend off a blow. McCoy's hand hovered in the air a moment before falling away in an eloquent impersonation of defeat.

'What's wrong?'

He crouched on the floor beside her and, though she drew away from him hastily, put his arm round her shoulder. He felt her small frame shudder as she began to sob. The story came out between the sobs – the story of how the others had been leaving pictures in her room, in the hall, on the toilet walls, everywhere, in places where they knew she'd find them, evil pictures meant for her. McCoy remembered the walls in the w.c. and asked:

'What kind of pictures?'

'I told you. Evil.'

'Yes but pictures of what?'

'Does it matter?'

'It might.' But it might not. They were evil and they were meant for her and she was unwilling to describe them.

She wiped the tears from her cheeks with the tips of her fingers. McCoy's hand, still on her shoulder, began to feel awkward. Soon it would have to retreat or go on to commit itself further. He looked at the hole in the ceiling.

'How did that happen?'

'I did it.'

'Why?'

'I could hear them upstairs, their voices. I couldn't make out what they were saying. I thought . . . they were trying to tell me something. Then the furniture started moving –'

'Moving?'

'Moving round the room, round my bed. That's why I put it out in the hall.'

'I see.'

She gave him a sidelong look. McCoy smiled encouragingly. He tried to squeeze her shoulder reassuringly, but his hand made it the wrong kind of squeeze. She seemed to ignore the hand as she said:

'D'you think I'm an easy lay?'

'I didn't mean that!'

'That's what they all say!'

'I'm sorry.'

'I want you to go now.'

McCoy, head in hands, the supplicant: 'Alison, I wasn't trying to do anything, honest. Listen, all this about the furniture moving and the voices trying to tell you things, I mean it's probably just the people up the stairs you can hear. I mean, thinking those pictures were meant for you, had messages for you, well, I think you need help, Alison, and maybe I can't help but maybe I can, but I can't if you don't trust me . . .'

Never had he sounded more sincere, but that was just the problem, the way the sounding it got in the way of the feeling it.

'Trust!' She spat the word at him a few times before continuing: 'I don't trust my friends, I don't trust the people I'm living with, I don't trust myself any more, so why the fuck should I trust you?'

'Because there's nobody left to trust,' said McCoy, hopefully.

'Trust.'

And she started to do what she'd done with 'curious' and 'cosy', repeating the word over and over again, with an edge of derision at first but then dreamily, as if trying to remember someone's face by repeating their name over and over again.

McCoy climbed to his feet.

'If you want me to go, I'll go.'

She said nothing. She didn't look at him as he put on his coat – still damp across the shoulders – but sat with her knees drawn up to her chin and her face turned to the wall. As he swung the haversack on to his shoulder, she spoke:

'There is something.' He turned to face her but she kept her face averted. 'If you want to help me, you can fit one of those things, those spy-holes, in the door.'

'It already has one.'

'This door.'

'You're crazy.'

'Maybe I am.'

He regretted saying it but couldn't find the words to unsay it. He stood in silence as she rummaged in the travel-bag. She pulled out a five-pound note.

73

'I'll pay you. How much do you want?'

McCoy refused the money haughtily.

'I won't do it, Alison.'

'Why not? My money's as good as anyone else's, isn't it?'

'Alison, I think a spy-hole in your bedroom door is the last thing you need. I mean, it already has holes in it anyway –'

'Please.'

Reluctantly he pulled the hand-drill from his bag and started drilling a hole in the door just below the painted-over window. When he'd fitted the spy-hole, he stooped to gather up the wood-shavings on the floor. Not knowing what to do with them, he let them fall to the floor again.

'How much do I owe you?'

'Don't insult me.'

She stood up and walked to the door to inspect his handiwork, pushing the fiver into his hand as she brushed past him. McCoy ordered his hand to give it back immediately, but his hand refused, and instead tightened its grip on the fiver and dived with it into his coat pocket, where it fondled it unashamedly in the dark.

She asked him to go outside the door so that she could try looking through the spy-hole. McCoy stood outside the door and saw the pinpoint of light through the spy-hole go dark as her eye came to it.

'Okay?'

There was no answer. The lock clicked, then the light in the room went out. He called her name, knocked on the door, rattled the handle. No response.

'I'll be on my way then, Alison.'

Silence.

'Have a good New Year, when it comes . . . Cheerio!'

The cheeriness of the word ill-befitted his mood or the occasion. He stalked along the hallway, out the door and up the stairs. The rain had subsided. Though it was still early in the day the light was strangely leaden, and heavy clouds over Edinburgh were general.

He thought again about the areas he had covered, that dark stain spreading over the street-map. Soon it would cover the city and all its sorry close-dwellers, then what?

Window-cleaning.

SHE POURED HERSELF a G and T, stubbed out her cigarette in the overflowing ash tray, lit another and dialled the next number. When she had let it ring half a dozen times and was on the point of hanging up, it was answered.

'Hello, I'm not sure if I've got the right number. Is there a Donald McDonald there?'

'Indeed. This is he.'

'The television producer?'

'I have been known to put the odd programme together, yes.'

'Thank God I've got you at last, I've been trying lots of numbers . . . they wouldn't give me your number – at STV, I mean. I mean, it's quite understandable, of course –' She felt herself beginning to prattle on.

'What can I do for you, my dear?'

'It's about *The Hogmanay Show*.'

'Oh yes?'

'Yes. It's about Pat McCoy, one of the acts.'

'McCoy . . . Oh, yes, the comedian – he is on the show. What about him?'

'Well, he's dead.'

She heard her own voice saying it but it still didn't make it real. The Producer sounded faintly irritated.

'Dead, is he? Oh bleeping hell, that's all I need. Are you absolutely sure?'

'Of course I'm sure. I'm his girlfriend –'

She heard the catch in her own voice as she said it.

'Oh my dear, I'm most dreadfully sorry. What a bleeping pity. And he was so young. What happened?'

'Suicide.'

75

'Oh good lord, how awful. Well, my dear, if there's anything I can do –'

She stifled a sob into the phone and said she was sorry in a squeaking voice. Donald McDonald was flustered.

'Oh, this really is terribly ah . . . Oh, bleep. Look my dear, I know how terribly upsetting this must be for you but, ah . . . really, I don't really see what, I mean to say . . . why are you telling me about all this?'

'Shouldn't it be announced, or something? Before the show comes on? I mean, his family could be watching, it could be upsetting –'

'Aha. I think I see what you're getting at. Oh bleeping hell.'

'Why d'you keep saying that?'

'Sorry, my dear, just a habit I picked up from my days with the Beeb.'

'Eh?'

'The bleeping.'

'Oh.'

'Now, anyway, you're absolutely right, of course. There will have to be an announcement. It might not be too late to edit him out –'

'Oh, don't do that –'

'Well, the problem is, you see, the show's meant to be live. Not much hope of preserving that time-honoured illusion if you've just announced that one of the performers is dead, if you follow me. No, I'm afraid I'll have to get on to Glasgow right away to see what can be done. Thank you very much indeed for informing me. It really is a dreadful nuisance – I mean, a terrible pity – or rather, a tragic waste . . .'

She stopped listening as the clichés of condolence oozed into her ear.

She said an abrupt goodbye and put the phone down. She reached for the gin. She might as well get pissed. Everyone else would be doing it, it wouldn't matter. It was the only thing to do.

She switched the t.v. on, then she switched it off again. She wandered around the flat, pulling clothes from the rail in the bedroom and throwing them on the bed. She resisted the temptation to look through old photographs and letters.

She changed into her jeans and her boots, brushed her hair, ate a piece of buttered toast and went to pour herself another gin but put the bottle back down before she opened it and reached for her coat instead. As if she had come to a decision. As if she was going out somewhere. As if she had somewhere to go.

HE TRIED A FEW more doors in the area with no success. He was on the point of throwing in the towel and going home, but the thought of the shed was enough to make him persevere. He had made two sales and both had been hard going. Though the rain was off, the streets were deep with slush and his feet were sodden. Remembering the shoes for sale, he decided to head for Tollcross trying a few doors on the way.

His luck turned at the first one that was answered: a thin, dark-haired man in his forties opened the door combing his hair. In the background loud blues music boomed from a stereo, so that McCoy had to raise his voice to make himself heard. The man, who was from Glasgow, was not at all surprised to see him at his door, and even cut McCoy's sales pitch short to say:

'That's handy, eh? Stick wan in, then.'

Though he was in the middle of getting ready to go out, knotting his tie and brushing his jacket, he hung around at the doorway, whistling and chatting to McCoy as he drilled the hole and fitted the spy-hole.

'Ah used tae do a bitty selling myself. Door-to-door. Ah was good, tae, but Ah got fed up wi it – aw, the thing is, even when you're good, you end up sellin yersel, eh no?'

McCoy nodded up from his work and changed the subject, which was too close to home for him.

'What are you doing tonight?'

'Gawn tae a pairty. Trouble is, every Saturday night's like New Year now, eh no?' he said as he inspected his lapels in the hall mirror. He went on: 'Naw. New Year's no the same as it used tae be. Ah member wan year – this is in Glasgow, mind you – Ah'd been at a pairty, know, Oh Christ Ah was steamin.

And Ah had ma big, daft donkey heid oan, know what Ah mean? Ah mean the day, even though it's New Year and that, Ah'm wearin ma sensible heid, know? Ah'll get blotto the night, but Ah'll no dae anythin crazy, because Ah've no got ma crazy heid oan, even although it's New Year. But this time, Oh Christ, Ah had ma big, daft dunkey heid oan, Ah was fuckin bananas.

So Ah gets intae the middle o the road – cars an aw that blarin their horns at me, know? – an first Ah takes aff ma tie an flings it in the air, then ma jaiket, then the shirt 'n the vest, then shoes, troosers, the lot. Ah mean, the lot – well, right doon tae ma wys. There Ah wis, runnin along Buchanan Street in the bare buff!'

'What happened?'

'Christ only knows. Ah woke up the next day in a cell charged wi indecent exposure! Indecent exposure! Ah coulda hud hypothermia! Guid joab a wis arrested! Ah couldnae even remember it! Ah still can't!'

McCoy listened to the man's story as he worked, feeling for the first time this day vaguely happy at his work: what was it about this man that made it all seem perfectly natural, even when he opened his wallet and paid McCoy, telling him to keep the change, as if the business transaction was neither here nor there but was instead all the excuse that was needed to make friends with somebody.

'Right you are, all the best when it comes anyway.' He nodded to McCoy with familiarity and even shook his hand before closing his door.

At the very next door, he made another quick sale, to a young couple who were in the process of painting their hall: the young man was wearing dungarees and his wife was wearing one of his old shirts and had her hair tied back with something. A radio on the floor was playing pop music and both looked happily engrossed in what they were doing. Through the open door to the living room McCoy could see a sleeping baby in a carry-cot on the floor. McCoy explained his mission with the cheerful confidence given to him by his last customer, avoiding all suggestion of threat and presenting the spy-hole as more of a household convenience, in case you didn't want to be troubled by Jehova's Witnesses or other tedious interruptions. The husband looked at his wife and there was some kind of mutual agreement which didn't require words, then the man told him to go ahead.

Half-way through the job, the baby woke up and started crying, and the woman put down her brush and went to see to it. The baby's cries grew louder and more frenzied, then the man put down his brush and went to help. McCoy could hear them making reassuring noises to the baby and discussing what might be the matter, but it was the baby's cries that were cutting through him.

What had she said to him at the party? That she might be. That she was late. She was sometimes late. It didn't mean she was. And what had he said?

'No idea who the father is, I suppose?'

Something like that no doubt. Oh Christ Yvonne forgive me. You know how I am. You know I didn't mean it. You know it wasn't me talking like that, you know it was the Other . . .

When he had finished the man came back out to the door, had a look at the spy-hole and paid him. It was definitely a good stair. On the second floor, though he didn't make a sale, the interest was there and people seemed to look at him sympathetically.

On the top floor, an old couple came out and again it was easy. He didn't expect to make the sale, so he didn't push it too hard, didn't bother with the Patter, and he could tell it was working because he was on top of it, it wasn't getting to him, it didn't matter if he made the sale or not, he didn't care any more, there was no desperation in his voice as he explained why the spy-hole was a good idea. The old couple looked worried, but didn't need much persuasion.

On the way out of the close, the man from Glasgow's words came back to him – you end up sellin yersel, eh no? – and he stopped before stepping out into the street to roll a cigarette.

If there was one thing that was sure to put people off, it was the feeling that you needed the sale. If they got a whiff of your true desperation, they shut their doors on you pronto. If you could be nonchalant, smiling, undaunted . . . Sometimes he could do it and sometimes he couldn't. It wasn't real anyway, it was all an act, but sometimes he could do the act and sometimes he couldn't. It was the same on stage. If they sensed that you needed the laugh, then by Christ they'd make you work for it. The same went for other things. Like if you really needed a place to stay, nothing was more likely to put people off giving you a bed for the night. If you had a bed to go to, on the other hand, a different story then.

Love was like that as well. It was there for you until you really needed it.

But he had made five sales, two of which he had been overpaid for, in one morning. It was incredible. Looked at in a purely business light, he had never had it so good. Two more sales and it would be a record day. It was the last day of the year, that must be what it was. People were in the mood for a diversion and were willing to let go of a few quid. He must make the most of this day, just as the taxi-drivers must. Yes, he would forego his official lunch-break and instead eat his rolls between closes, between customers. By Christ he would pay his debts before the year was out and no mistake. Semple would get his filthy wad of greenbacks to see in the New Year with yet.

And he would get his bottle.

So steeling himself to keep going, McCoy came to a busy street near Haymarket and crossed the road heading for Tollcross. As he did he saw Jan Pringle, one of the teachers from Yvonne's school, walking over the road towards him. He greeted her in passing with a cheery sideways nod of the head, only to see her drop her bag in the middle of the road and freeze.

McCoy didn't move either, apart from swaying uneasily from side to side, because he was feeling it again, even though he wasn't up there in the spotlight, even though there was no audience there. Like giving yourself the slip. Like stepping inside the Other. Like being tried on. Like being somebody else's overcoat.

As she stooped to pick up the bag – the lights were about to change – her eyes locked on McCoy.

Thinking that Yvonne had told her the story of the row at the party the night before last, McCoy caught her arm as she made to hurry past and, hearing a car peep its horn at them, retraced his steps with her to the side of the road.

'Jan – how are you doing? Did you not recognise me?'

She seemed to watch his lips as he spoke, as if having to lip-read.

'Hello Pat – sorry, I'm half-blind without my contacts.' She blinked her eyes rapidly. 'I know – we met that night at *Hamlet*, eh?'

81

And it had been at *Hamlet*. One of the godawful school outings Yvonne had dragged him along to, along with a couple of the other teachers and a busload of dressed-up teenagers who had heckled poor Hamlet's too too sullied flesh to smithereens.

'Oh God, that's right,' said McCoy. 'Remember when Hamlet was comparing the locket of his father to the other one of what's-his-name –'

'Claudius.'

'Right, and that poor ham, oh Christ I felt for him when he threw the one of Claudius too far and it rolled off the stage –'

'That's right, and then he had to pick it up again later on in the soliloquy, didn't he?'

'Oh God yes, and then when that locket came rolling back on stage from the wings and all the kids started giving it the slow hand clap and Hamlet started telling them to shut up . . . it was priceless!'

'It was pretty dreadful, wasn't it?'

More rapidly blinking eyes and this time, a smile. But even her smile seemed to conceal something, something she knew and he didn't.

'Are you all right?' she asked him.

McCoy shrugged. 'Could be worse, I suppose.'

'You're not ill, or anything?'

'I had a bad hangover after Hugh's party. I'm okay now. Why?'

'Nothing. I thought I heard that you were ill, or something.'

'It's news to me,' said McCoy. 'Who told you I was ill?'

'It was just something Maggie Jordan said . . . she must've got you mixed up with somebody else.'

'Maggie Jordan . . . I think I've met her . . . who is she?'

'She's new. In Yvonne's department. She's going out with Tony McTaggart.'

'Is that right? I met Tony the other night, but Maggie Jordan . . . I think I maybe met her once. What did she say?'

'Nothing. I can't really remember. Anyway, you're okay, so it doesn't really matter, does it?'

She smiled at him indulgently. McCoy smiled back at her and for a moment they stood there on the corner of the street smiling stupidly at each other.

'You haven't seen Yvonne, have you?' enquired McCoy, with what he hoped was nonchalance.

'Not since the end of term – why? Have you not seen her yourself?'

'Oh yes, I saw her the other night,' said McCoy. 'I just wondered if you'd maybe bumped into her or something – today, I mean.'

'No, should I have?'

'No, I just wondered.'

'I should imagine she'll probably go to Tony's party. Will you not be going?'

'I think so.'

She gave him a puzzled look as she drew away from him.

'I'd better go – I'll maybe see you at the party, eh?'

'In case I don't get there –' He caught her by the shoulder and gave her a kiss on the cheek, but though she allowed her cheek to be kissed, he could feel her pulling away and thought he detected a shudder of repulsion.

'Happy New Year, when it comes!' he called to her as she walked away.

The way she'd dropped her bag, as if the very sight of him . . . the way she'd shuddered when he'd kissed her . . . McCoy eyed his reflection in the glass of the shop windows as he passed them. Was he so repulsive? He looked rough. But not rough enough to make somebody drop their bag. And then, what was this about Maggie Jordan? She was in the same department as Yvonne and that didn't bode well. And she was going out with Tony McTaggart, but he felt sure that Tony had been on his own at the party the other night. And there was something else, something worse . . . Maggie Jordan, the name was making something rise to the surface of his memory, something that didn't want to come to the surface, something that wanted to stay in the black hole of his forgetfulness . . .

The only time he had met her, now that he thought about it, had been in the pub with Yvonne and the other teachers, just before Christmas, on the last day of the term. He couldn't remember much about her. Young. Fair hair. Skinny. A bit innocent, a bit gullible. Teaching would soon knock that out of her . . .

83

He was relieved of his thoughts by the apparition of a No. 2 bus, which he had to run to catch. He got off at Bread Street, where he cut through a vennel behind the tenements and came upon a young man crouched by the wall, vomiting over the cobbles. So it had started already. McCoy had got the worst part of the ritual over with a day early. There would be a lot more of it to come, gallons of spewed beer and puked-up carry-out kebabs, fetid fish suppers and half-chewed chop sueys. There would be dark red rum-and-coke retches and colourless, viscous vodka vomits, little dry sicks and big wet eruptions bespattering the streets of Scotland everywhere, gobbed up in gutters, splattered in shop doorways, coughed into the niches of statues, sprayed over flowerbeds, retched under hedges, boked up in bus-shelters, trailed over windowsills, gagged against gravestones, skooshed on country roads from the windows of veering cars, honked from high bridges, blocking toilet bowls and plugholes all over the land. It all had to come out, all the despair and the futility of the year, the decade, the century, in a communal orgy of regurgitation.

'Eh . . . are you okay?'

The young man opened his mouth to speak but quickly turned away to heave more of the contents of his stomach onto the cobbles, waving McCoy away with a hand as he did so.

McCoy walked up to Tollcross, eating his ham roll on the way – he'd keep the other for later – sensing with deepening dread the looming celebration. Though it was early in the day, already people were hurrying through the streets with intent, serious faces.

As he passed a pub, its door swung open and closed as someone went in. The smell of the beer and the sounds of the television and the voices came out to meet him. It was warm in there. There were people to talk to. Pies to eat. Pints to drink. It was another world in there.

I must not. It would be a mistake. Starting this early in the day. It would be a disaster.

IT WAS BUSY. A swift half was what was needed. Though many men would scorn a half-pint, he knew that in his case it was neither a half-pint of moderation nor a half-pint of caution, but a half-pint of necessity, a half-pint of weakness, a half-pint of desperation.

He recognised no one, though many of the congregation looked over at him as he made his way from the door to the bar. The haversack drew one or two looks: who did he think he was, a worker?

He did his best to look like one.

Out of habit, he ordered a pint. It was the last day of the year. He asked the young, long-nosed barman if he had anything to eat.

'Just reheated leftovers,' he said, cheerfully, 'or pies.'

He ordered a pie. He saw a seat at the far end of the bar and carried his pie and his pint there.

'Is anybody there?' he asked, pointing to the free place. One of the two young girls sitting at the table looked up at him and shook her head.

He drank some of the beer, ate his pie and looked at the light coming through the stained glass of the windows and reflected in the big mirrors, till in one of these he saw the reflection of a face he knew so well that he could have sworn it was Sandra Burnett – an old, old flame from Bonnyrigg.

She had swept past him to go to the ladies before he had a chance to look at her again. He turned in his chair to get a better view of the doorway to the ladies, so that he could see her properly when she came out.

Sandra Burnett. Christ.

She was not his first love. Love it had not been, not even the illusion of love. No, he could not kid himself on that score.

85

His first love had been Pauline, Platonic to the last despite his fumbling attempts – or, maybe, because of these – at seduction.

Sandra Burnett had come later. Having nowhere to go, they had done it anywhere they could think of: behind the trees in the park in the cold; in derelict buildings and dark side-streets, in doorways and car-parks; sometimes in her own garden, after he'd walked her home, before she went in to meet her father, who was the chief of police for the area. More often they had gone to the place they thought of as theirs, because it was the place where they had screwed each other for the first time: the graveyard. Those uneven graves like unmade beds, as if the dead were restless.

The only time they had been caught at it had been there – by the organist. They had sometimes been able to hear him practising for the service the next day as they shuddered together in the vestibule area of the church, behind the stone statues of a king and queen.

She came out of the ladies, he saw that it really was her and he rose from his chair to meet her.

'Sandra.'

'Oh my God, Pat McCoy.'

She looked unpleasantly surprised to see him. Before she could say anything, he kissed her cheek and pulled his chair out for her. She sat down on the edge of it and looked worried as he went off to find another chair for himself.

'Fancy meeting you in here!' She laughed the way she had always laughed: scornfully, with a hand over her mouth, as if she didn't know how to laugh.

'Sandra Burnett. Are you with anybody?'

'You mean here, or in general?' she said, defensively.

'Here,' said McCoy, feeling his nostrils twitch as he said it and remembering how she had always made his nostrils twitch.

She nodded and pointed to a table at the other end of the bar where a group of women her age were laughing and talking animatedly.

'They work beside me.'

He didn't pursue it: 'It's good to see you again, Sandra.'

'Well, how come you look so bored about it then? It's a co-incidence. It is. To meet like this – well, don't you think so?'

'Incredible,' said McCoy, and he could feel himself sliding into some half-remembered routine with her.

'You haven't changed!'

'Neither have you, Sandra.'

'I have so.'

'Oh yeah? How?'

She gave him an outraged look he had always found flattering and laughed again, then pressed her lips together in a way he had always found incredibly sexy. He didn't want to speak to her until he had time to savour more of those details. She had changed. She had the same dry, straw-blonde hair but now it was cut short. Her face looked thinner and there were a few wrinkles around her green eyes, but the overall effect of these changes was that the gawky girl he had known had matured to a winsome beauty. And, of course, her clothes had changed: no longer the cheap and fashionable fripperies of nylon, viscose and courtelle; now it was the leather and cashmere of a single woman with a salary. The business of the clothes bothered him: his own, compared to hers. Power dressing. McCoy had heard of it.

Still every move she made sent out its signal to him just as it had all those years ago, when they had gone nowhere together for a few months. Old longings stirred McCoy, complicated by a new curiosity: would it be the same, now?

'I'm still here, you know,' she said, giving him a wide-eyed look just in the way she had done then, except that now it looked more deliberate.

'So you are,' he said.

'Well, speak to me for heaven's sake!'

'I just want to look at you for a minute.'

This flattered and embarrassed her so much that she had to laugh again, though she did not want to laugh, because she had never liked her own voice. It was the kind of voice that sounded ill at ease with itself. It kept changing its tone and its pitch unpredictably, veering from a barely audible and tentative whine to a screechy laugh. When she meant to whisper, her voice croaked. When she intended to speak evenly and thoughtfully, it blurted out an opinion or added an edge of something – sarcasm, frivolity or guile. That was the important thing to get right when he did her – and he remembered doing her a lot

87

in the past, to make her laugh, laugh at herself, laugh at her own laughter.

Imposing a minute of silence on her was just the kind of thing he would have done then, to tease her, to put her through the ordeal of her laughter, but now he knew what he was doing and didn't enjoy it as much.

'Remember the organist's face,' said McCoy, then, impersonating that intruder from the past: 'Ye should be downright ashamed o yersels, oan consecratit grund! Ye'll roast in the fires o hell!'

She thought better of laughing at that and acted none too pleased to be reminded of her squandered virginity with him. So McCoy laughed his most infectious laugh, the one reserved for difficult audiences. She had been a difficult audience for him then and now nothing had changed except that they knew it and they were eating the reheated leftovers.

At last she capitulated with a laugh that was a bit of a snarl as well.

She told him she was working as a teacher in Dalkeith and shared a flat in Portobello with two other teachers. She wasn't married. The fact that she had become a teacher depressed him. Everybody had become a teacher.

What about him? What was he doing?

The question was one he instinctively evaded, glossing over the years between who he had been and who he had become as quickly as he could, leaving out his personal life entirely, as if it was a series of stage appearances, from his first walk-on one-liner in a comedy sketch, through the stand-up spots in clubs and at godforsaken functions to the high point of the present day and his forthcoming triumphant appearance on *The Hogmanay Show*.

'Really?' She looked as if she believed him but didn't want to. 'You mean, like Andy Stewart, imitating Elvis?'

'Well, no, my act's a bit different –'

'You're what they call an alternative comedian, is that it?'

'Alternative to what?'

'You tell me.'

'I don't believe in the label. Maybe all comedians are alternative. They've no alternative.'

He was aware that she was looking at his coat, the haversack over the chair, his shoes. No, he had not made good.

'D'you ever go back out to Bonnyrigg?'

'Just to see my mum. I don't know anybody there any more. I used to go back more before my old man died –'

'Oh, I didn't know he was dead. I'm sorry, Pat.' she said.

'Oh, yeah. Well that was a a couple of years ago now,' said McCoy, uncomfortably. He could not remember exactly when.

'It must've been a shock.'

'Well, not really, he'd been ill for quite a while –'

He regretted that the death had come up, since it was too intimate a thing to talk about. They had never talked about anything serious when he'd gone out with her. Conversation between them had always been verbal foreplay – she resisted all his approaches until he made her laugh. He was on the point of asking her if she knew Yvonne, to change the subject, when he noticed that she was leaning forward in her seat a little and looking at him with a puzzled frown.

'What are you looking at me like that for, Sandra?'

'Nothing.'

But her voice underlined it too heavily and he knew that there was something.

'Come on, Sandra, you can tell me.'

'I just remembered something you said to me, once. I just remembered you saying . . . that you'd never be free, until your dad died.'

'Until what?'

'Until your father died.'

'I never said that!'

'You did, Pat, I remember it.'

'I can't believe I said that.' But he could. It was exactly the kind of thing he would have said to her when he was seventeen, for effect, to try to shock or impress her. Now it embarrassed him and he felt obliged to deny it:

'I can't remember saying anything like that.'

'You did, that's what you said.'

'When?'

'I don't know, do I? You don't expect me to remember everything, do you?'

'No, but –'

But it seemed that she did: after a moment she told him that he'd said it one night in her house when her parents had gone away for the night, the only night they had shared a bed.

'You remember that, eh?' she said, defying him not to and defying him to remember it as well with the same sharp glance of her green eyes.

It was just like Sandra Burnett to get on to him about something he had said to her fifteen years ago.

'Well, even if I did say that. So what?'

'Well . . . are you?'

McCoy felt himself flush like a blundering teenager. Sandra smiled with satisfaction – she had seldom shocked or embarrassed him in the past – it had usually worked the other way.

'Sandy, that was just the kind of thing I said when I was seventeen. I said anything then, I didn't think about it . . .'

'D'you think about what you say now?'

'Well, I think so . . . Anyway, freedom and all that, I don't think about that kind of stuff now . . .'

'Do you not?'

'Well, even if I do, I don't go around talking like that – freedom, Christ Almighty Sandra, maybe I'm free but what good's it done me?'

She ran her eyes over him, over his clothes. He thought that she looked a little disappointed with him.

'Maybe you were right.'

'How d'you mean?'

'What you said then. You wouldn't say it now, but maybe that's because you're not as –'

'Not as what?' said McCoy, sounding more worried than he'd meant to. How had the conversation, which should have been a matter of fond memories, and maybe a bit of nostalgic flirtation, taken this wrong turn? 'I thought you said I hadn't changed.'

'I know, but –' She shrugged, smiled and looked over to her friends at the other end of the bar. 'I mean even if you did say it to impress me, maybe it was still true. I mean, you can't just dismiss it like that.'

'It might be true, but I don't think so, somehow. Somehow I don't think the dead go away as easy as that. The dialogue goes on – or, in the case of my old man, the monologue.'

90

She didn't seem impressed. She had learnt how to narrow her eyes. In the old days they'd screwed each other in eager and ignorant bliss and everything surrounding their childlike acts of fornication had been subsidiary. After Pauline, Sandra had been refreshingly straightforward, but now she had learnt how to narrow her eyes and, who knows, if they were to make love now she might narrow them during it, or afterwards, snatching impatiently on her cigarette, the way she was doing now.

'What are you doing tonight, Sandra?'

She gave him a dirty look, as if he was asking her out.

'We're having a party,' she said, nodding to her friends at the far end of the bar. 'How about you?'

McCoy shrugged. 'I won't be going to the Tron this year, that's for sure.'

'You'd miss yourself on the telly, eh?'

'It's not that. I don't even want to see myself that much. I'd rather skip New Year altogether, to tell you the truth, but I'll probably end up at a party somewhere . . .' A moment of toil as he waited for the invitation. Eventually it came: 'Come to ours, if you want.'

'Thanks, Sandra, I might –'

He gave her the Christmas card to write down the address.

'What's this – another party?' she asked him, pointing at the address in Tarvit Street.

'Yeah,' he lied, 'but I might come to yours instead.'

But it wasn't on. Apart from anything else, she lived in Portobello. He didn't want to get stuck in Portobello at New Year. It would be a party of teachers. There would be somebody there who knew Yvonne, there would be sure to be. Anyway, he could tell by the way she was writing the address that she didn't really want him to come.

She glanced at the Nativity scene on the card and grimaced before handing it to him.

As she moved in her seat, the haversack swung against her leg.

'What's in here? Your kerry-oot?'

'Wish it was,' said McCoy, wishing it was. He told her the pitiful story of how he was trying to make the rent. It worked. She opened her bag, took out her purse and gave him a ten.

'It won't be enough, but maybe it'll help,' she said.

91

'I can't take it,' protested McCoy, not too adamantly.

'Why not? You paid me into the pictures often enough.'

'Did I? Oh well . . . thanks, Sandra, you're a pal.'

He took it quickly and crumpled it in his hand.

'Well, I'd better get back. Come along tonight, if you feel like it.'

McCoy nodded. 'If I don't make it, Happy New Year, Sandra –'

He kissed her too urgently and held her too tight and he felt her pulling away from him. She patted his arm with her hand as she did and smiled. She was pleased. She had come out on top.

'I'd better go.'

McCoy watched her go to her friends. It looked like they were quizzing her about him and he thought he heard his old flame's scornful laugh as she answered them. He told himself that when she sounded scornful it meant she wasn't. He told himself that it wasn't really him they were talking about. It was some other McCoy, long since dead and buried, if he had ever really existed.

He looked at his glass. Though he longed for another he didn't want to sit here alone, with her at the other end of the bar. He picked up the Christmas card and checked the number in Tarvit Street before putting it back in his pocket.

Sandra Burnett. Christ.

He drank up and left through the lounge bar so that he wouldn't have to pass her on the way out.

WHEN HE FOUND the stair, he made his way up but stopped at the second-floor landing to get his breath and have a smoke. As he smoked he leaned over the bannister, looking down into the dark stair-well.

A tenner. Would he pay for them with the tenner his mother had sent him, or the one Sandra Burnett had given him, or with ten quid of the money he'd earned? Did it matter?

It would have to be his mother's tenner. How come money had to come to him in this way? Why couldn't it just be anonymous money, the kind most people earned? Even the stuff he'd been paid came stamped indelibly with the head of Mrs Bernard or had been touched by the girl in the box-room. It wasn't clean money. It was dirty money. It smelled of humanity. It was disgusting. The main thing was to get rid of it as soon as possible.

Ten pounds. O.n.o.

Somehow that o.n.o. spoke of desperation, but then he was desperate as well. The way Sandra Burnett had looked him over like that . . . something had to be done. He needed a decent pair of shoes and these certainly sounded all right. Unworn. He was a bit suspicious of the 'not imperfect'. It probably meant there was something wrong with them and, now that he remembered the wording of the ad., he realised that there had been no mention of the colour. Lime-green oxford brogues? On the other hand, he needed a pair of shoes urgently. It was worth a try. But if he didn't like them or they didn't fit, how would he say no? He found that hard enough when he tried on shoes in shoe shops. How much more difficult would it be trying on a pair in somebody's house, somebody who really needed to sell them?

His prevarication about the shoes was interrupted when

someone came into the stair and ran up them two at a time. McCoy turned to go back down, then recognised the balding head, the dark, mournful eyes and the permanently worried frown of Willie Turnbull as he panted level with him.

'Willie. How are you doing?'

'Aw, so-so, Pat. You?'

'Oh, not so good. It's a bad time of year to be skint.'

'Aye, the worst. So what brings you up this way?'

It was the way they always opened a conversation with each other, as if they were afraid to admit that anything in their lives might be as it should be. McCoy admitted to the spy-hole selling but not to the advert for the shoes.

'Want a cup of tea?' said Willie.

'You mean you live here? I thought you lived down Leith?'

'Aye, we had to move. Been here nearly a year.'

'Is that right? I didn't know.'

Willie shook his head, as if the move from Leith was the latest confirmation of how terrible things were. McCoy followed him up to his door. It was only when he saw Willie's name on the door that it chimed in his brain with the name on the card in the grocer's window. Turnbull. So Willie was selling his shoes.

McCoy had met Willie Turnbull at a function in Tranent years ago, where he had been doing a spot and Willie had been hired to take photographs. It had been a typical small-town function-suite nightmare of the office party variety, and though McCoy had made them laugh, the experience had depressed him. He had met Willie at the bar and they had got gloomily drunk together at a corner table while the partygoers whooped it up around them.

He had met him from time to time over the years since then, at parties or in pubs, or in the queue to sign on. He had never got to know him well, never set foot in his flat before, but he had always nodded to him in the street and sometimes stopped to have a bit of a conversation, which usually took the form of mutual commiseration about the way things were in general.

Just inside the door there were stepladders, a bike, a pram, a disused washing machine and a mound of coats on a sideboard. It was a very small and very cluttered flat.

'Are Lynne and the boy in?' McCoy asked.

'They're away to the granny's. Lynne's old man was buried last week there. She's due back any minute.' He led him into a tiny

94

kitchen, filled the kettle and told him to have a seat.

'So you're goin round the doors, Pat? Make much?' McCoy sagged into the chair and shook his head. 'Aye. it's hard to sell anythin door-to-door. I've tried it myself. Encyclopedias. This was in London, mind you. You meet a lot of folk, though, eh?'

McCoy nodded and squinted at Willie's feet to see if he was wearing the shoes, but the pair he had on were black.

'And when you did get a sale you made quite a bit . . . Are you still doin the clubs?'

'Now and again. I'm trying to get away from them, to tell you the truth Willie. I'm on telly tonight.'

Willie sat down opposite McCoy and looked at him worriedly. He was used to failure and any whiff of success made him uneasy.

'Is that right?'

'*The Hogmanay Show*. Just before the bells. A five-minute spot. Try and catch it, Willie.'

'Oh, definitely. I bet that pays okay, eh?'

'Well, I think it will. I don't know, I haven't been paid yet.' Willie looked relieved and nodded. 'It should come in soon, it was recorded in October. How about you, Willie, are you working?' Willie shook his head and covered his mouth with a hand. 'Still taking pictures on the side?'

Willie shook his head again and twisted his mouth into a grimace.

'I got had up for it a long time ago. At a Freemason's Christmas dinner in Penicuik.'

'Who told on you?'

'Aw, this bastard I was renting my flat from was there. I'm sure it was him, he tried to blackmail me.'

'Aw come on, Willie, he didn't.'

'Well, he doubled the rent and when I said I'd take him to the Rent Tribunal he let me know he'd been at the do in Penicuik. When I found somewhere else, I was hauled in and that was me.'

'For fuck sake,' McCoy said, sympathetically, 'was that why you moved here?'

'Naw, this was years ago. This was when I was renting a place from this guy Semple.'

'Not George Semple?'

Willie shrugged. 'I never knew his first name.'

95

'Did he run that big second-hand furniture place down Leith Walk?'

'Aye, that's the one. He's got a couple of antique shops as well – he's no just a junk-merchant. How? Have you met him?'

'He's my landlord,' said McCoy.

'Get away.'

'He is.'

Willie rolled his eyes in horror.

'I'd watch it, if I was you, Pat, that guy's bad news. Don't let him find out anything about you. I'm sure it was him that shopped me. The thing is as well, it was him that hired me to take the photographs. That's the kind of guy we're talkin about. He'd shop his granny. He's a Mason, and he's got a finger in a few pies. Owns a big place in Dublin Street, I mean it's a complete building, four floors, and rents it out to folk signing on. The conditions are terrible. There was a scandal in the paper about it. He's rakin it in.'

'What number Dublin Street?'

'I donno.'

'I live just round from there. Dublin Mews.'

Willie laughed ruefully and said: 'Aw aye – in thon shed?' McCoy nodded. 'I get to use the cellar of the building next to the shed. Mibbe that's the one you're talkin about.'

'That'll be it. Naw, I've steered clear of him since I moved out of Great Junction Street and I've stopped takin pictures on the side.'

'Did they take you to court, Willie?'

'Naw, but they nearly did. They were threatening to. They made me pay back the money. It's no worth the risk.'

'Christ,' said McCoy, 'I hope he doesn't watch *The Hogmanay Show*.'

'Who, Semple? How, has he got somethin on you?'

'Well, not really, but I'm a bit behind with the rent.'

Willie looked at McCoy as if his days were numbered, shook his head, and rose to make the tea.

McCoy waited for a minute, then said, 'Willie, are you selling a pair of shoes, by any chance?'

Willie turned round and put the tea-pot on the table. He looked flustered. McCoy grinned at him.

'Me? How?'

'I saw the card in Laird's.'

'Oh, did you?'

He looked at the floor in embarrassment.

'I was on the way to see the shoes when I met you.'

Willie looked up and nodded.

'Righto. I'll go and get them. They're a good pair of shoes.' Suddenly his movements were brisk and businesslike. He went out into the hallway. McCoy heard him rummaging in a cupboard, then he came back in and put the shoes down on the table, sat down and poured the tea.

McCoy looked at the shoes but didn't touch them as yet. They were a darker tan than the pair he had on, but still not the right colour for a stage appearance. He could see that they weren't real brogues, but imitation brogues, and couldn't have cost that much new. But they did look new and there didn't seem to be anything wrong with them.

'Try them on, Pat.'

McCoy nodded and picked up one of the shoes and looked at it from various angles. It would be harder to refuse them if he tried them on. It would be hard enough as it was.

'I don't know, Willie, I'm not that keen on the colour.'

'They're about the same as the pair you've got on.'

'A bit darker, but I've never been keen on tan –'

'You could dye them no bother, Pat, they're a perfectly good pair of shoes, they'd cost you at least twenty quid new.' McCoy pursed his lips judiciously.

'You didn't buy them, then?'

Willie faltered before saying, 'Well, no, Lynne got me them, but they're just a wee bit on the neat side for me, you know, I've got a broad foot. Try them, Pat, they're worth more than a ten-spot –'

'They're a good pair of shoes all right, but the thing is I usually take an eight-and-a-half or sometimes even a nine –'

'You won't know if they fit till you try them –'

To McCoy's horror, Willie jumped up from his chair, raked through a drawer, pulled out a shoe-horn and knelt at his feet.

'They're in better shape than them anyway,' he remarked, nodding at the shoes McCoy was wearing.

He made to untie McCoy's lace. McCoy intervened and did it himself, embarrassed and confused by the sight of his friend

97

kneeling at his feet and by the state of his own footwear. As he tugged his shoes off Willie sat back and let out a low whistle at the condition of McCoy's socks, which were soaked.

'Hold it right there,' said Willie, and he hurried out of the kitchen, returning a moment later with a pair of dry socks. 'I'll throw these in with the price of the shoes,' he said.

McCoy unpeeled his dishcloths and donned the fresh socks.

'I feel like a new man already,' he said. He wiggled his toes, then squeezed his feet into the imitation brogues – they felt a bit tight – and laced them up. He stood up and began pacing up and down in the small kitchen.

'How do they feel?'

'I don't know, Willie, they feel a bit tight.'

'They'll give. You have to break brogues in.'

'How come you didn't break them in?'

'I would have, I was going to, but it's the closed front, Pat, I've got too broad a foot, and they didn't look right on me. They look good on you, though, straight up. Dead smart.'

'I know, I know.' He paced up and down some more.

'Will I get a wee mirror?'

McCoy wouldn't hear of the idea. He sat down and made to unlace the shoes, but Willie stopped him.

'Keep them on for a bit. Get the feel of them. Finish your tea. Unless you fancy a wee nip?'

'Christ no, Willie, I'm still shakey from last night,' said McCoy, forgetting to mention that he'd already had a pint.

'Best thing for it. Haira the dug.'

McCoy wavered in his resolve and nodded with resignation.

'Just a wee one, mind.'

'It'll have to be,' said Willie, opening a cupboard door and pulling an almost empty half-bottle from a shelf. 'I'll have to get the drinks in later. What are you doing for it?'

'What?'

'New Year.'

'To tell you the truth, I don't know yet Willie. I wouldn't mind giving the whole thing a miss –'

'You'll want to watch yourself on telly, eh?'

'I suppose so.'

'I'll make a point of trying to see you. Here's to it.' He handed him a small tumbler of whisky. McCoy sipped at it gingerly, winced at the taste, then downed it and shook his head energetically.

'That better?'

'I think so.'

And it was. He felt a warmth spreading inside him. He stood up and walked up and down the kitchen, looking at the shoes this way and that. They began to look not too bad.

'They look dead good,' said Willie, 'honest.'

'It's the colour though, Willie, I've never been keen on the tan.'

'The pair ye're wearin are tan, Pat.'

'I know, but I've never liked them that much.'

'These are a much better made pair of shoes,' said Willie.

'They're a bit on the tight side as well,' said McCoy.

'They'll give, I'm telling you, and as for the colour, you could dye them black no bother. Tell you what, Pat, I'll let them go for eight. How's that?'

'It's not that,' said McCoy, 'they're worth the ten, but –'

'Never mind, save yourself a couple of quid, take them for eight,' urged Willie.

'I suppose they will give a bit.'

'Of course they'll give.'

He poured the last drops of the whisky into their glasses.

'What are you doing for it?' said McCoy, sitting back down at the table but still with his eyes on his feet.

'Just stayin in. A few folk comin by. Drop in, if you want, Pat, you're very welcome.'

'I'll see,' said McCoy, 'it depends how it goes – you know what New Year's like.'

Willie nodded his head.

'Ah remember one year, at the Tron. I climbed up into the Christmas tree in front of the Cathedral there –'

'For fuck sake, Willie, you did not.'

Willie shook his head and smiled at the memory.

'Oh Christ, Lynne was not pleased –'

'That's one place I won't be going this year,' said McCoy, before Willie could get too involved in the story of the New Year he'd climbed the christmas tree in front of St Giles.

He looked at the shoes he had taken off and realised that now that they had been replaced, if only for a few minutes, there was no going back to them.

99

'Eight quid, you say? Okay, I'll take them.'

'Great,' said Willie. 'I'll put them in a bag for you.'

McCoy stopped him before he got out of his seat.

'I'll just keep them on, Willie,' said McCoy, 'and you can throw those bastards in the bucket,' he added, nodding to his old shoes.

'Right you are,' said Willie, with a worried smile.

McCoy finished off his whisky, counted out the money and handed it to his friend. The sight of it made Willie look, if anything, more worried.

'Fancy a swift half-pint, Pat?'

'No,' said McCoy, unable to conceal the note of panic in his voice. 'I've got to get going.'

Willie nodded and saw him out to the door, where he invited McCoy again to drop in for the bells if he was in the area.

'If I'm in the area, I will. Anyway, all the best when it comes!'

While they were saying goodbye, Willie's wife Lynne came up the stairs carrying their two-year-old boy and a plastic bag of shopping.

'Not a word about the shoes,' he whispered to McCoy, as Lynne reached the landing and groaned wearily. She was surprised to see McCoy but was too out of breath to speak at first.

'Here, I'll take the bag,' offered Willie.

Lynne pushed her fair, thin hair away from her eyes and said, 'You can take him as well.'

Willie took the boy in his arms and told him to say hello to McCoy, but the boy hid his head in his father's shoulder.

McCoy said hello to the boy, asked Lynne how she was doing and moved from foot to foot, anxious to get away from this family gathering. He could sense that something wasn't right between Willie and his wife.

'We're havin some folk round –' began Lynne, but broke off abruptly when she saw the shoes. She gave Willie a penetrating look and said: 'What in hell's name do you think you're doin?'

Willie looked flustered. 'Pat needed a pair o shoes, Lynne, they were no good to me.'

'That's not the point, they're not even your shoes to give away!'

'I paid for them!' said McCoy.

'Aw that's right. On you go, land me in the shit,' said Willie to McCoy, 'you and Semple should get along fine. Shop your granny.'

'Christ Willie, whose shoes are they?'

At this, the boy turned his face from its hiding place in Willie's shoulder, looked down at McCoy's feet and said, 'Grandad's!'

'He only died last week,' said Lynne, with a bitter curl of her lip.

'Oh Christ, Lynne,' said McCoy, 'Willie didn't tell me they were his –'

'He doesnae need them any mair, does he?' said Willie, the appeal in his voice making it go high.

'I'll take them off right now,' said McCoy.

'No,' said Lynne with a resigned shake of her head, 'you might as well have them, Pat. But he shouldn't have charged you for them. That's not nice.'

Willie opened his mouth to speak, but his wife gave him a look that silenced him. She turned to McCoy and said, 'How much?'

'Eight quid, but it's okay, Lynne –'

'They're worth twenty anyway,' put in Willie.

Lynne ignored him and turned to McCoy. 'First he sells his books, then his radio, now his shoes – he'd just got them the day before he died – and I don't see a penny of it. It goes down his throat before I know he's got it.'

Willie interrupted her: 'C'mon now Lynne, this is nothin to do wi Pat, leave him out of this.'

Lynne had taken her purse out of her pocket and had counted out eight pounds, which she now tried to force on McCoy.

'No, no,' protested McCoy, 'I couldn't take it!' But she was a determined woman. She shoved it into the top pocket of McCoy's coat.

'I feel really bad about all this,' said McCoy.

'It's not your fault,' said Lynne, giving Willie another dirty look.

'Aw c'mon,' said Willie, 'it's the last day of the year, let's not argue, eh?'

His wife exhaled with exasperation, rolled her eyes and said to McCoy: 'Aye, I was goin to say. Come round tonight, Pat, we're havin a few folk round –'

'Aye,' said Willie, 'you're very welcome, Pat!'

101

It was his cue to get the hell away.

'If I'm in the area, I'll definitely look in. All the best when it comes anyway, eh?'

But he knew that he definitely wouldn't. The business of the shoes had embarrassed everybody. In many ways, it had been an ideal transaction, cutting out the long chain of middle-men, until he'd found out whose the shoes were and that Willie was trying to raise his beer money.

Outside, he stamped his feet once or twice to let the dead man's new shoes know who they were dealing with. They pinched his feet back. They were definitely a bit on the tight side.

He walked round the corner to Tollcross and looked at the clock: ten to four. Soon it would be getting dark. He could try a few more doors, but there was no point. He would never have enough money to pay Semple what he owed him. As it was, the money he had was burning a hole in his pocket. If he didn't give it to Semple he would give it to Victoria Wines or Scottish & Newcastle. He had to straighten something out with Semple, had to persuade him to give him another week's grace.

He crossed the road to a bus stop and waited for a bus to take him down Leith.

THE SUDDEN LUNGE of the bus as it left the stop sent him skidding along the upstairs aisle, grabbing for a handhold. He veered into a seat and was thrown from side to side as the driver communicated the urgency of the journey to his passengers in the jolt and screech of the brakes, in the rasp of the horn and the wild swerve as he took a corner too fast. Belting along Princes Street, there was barely the time to notice that the castle was lit up like a post-card of itself.

This driver was in a hurry. You'd think he was doing one of those tourist tours of the city . . .

Guid evenin, lassies an laddies! An welcome tae the fleein-sicht-seein stourin-roon-the-toon-tour o Auld Reekie, every fifteen meenits as it says aw owre the side o the bus! Youz eedjits oan the upstairs o the bus, stoap yer complainin – It's no meant tae hae a roof! Cauld? Of course it's cauld, that's pert and percel o the hale shebang, the Scottish Experience ye ken! Haud oan tae yer Nikkons ticht, fur wur no gonnae be hinging aboot owre lang onywhaur! An if yez want a translation o whit Ah'm sayin, turn the wee knab oan yer heid set anti-cloakwise tae settin yin, if ye want English, twa, if ye want American an three, if it's a guid auld bit o electric bagpipe music ye're efter! Jean, oor bonny wee Heighland bus-hostesse in the mini-kilt, 'll be roon wi the heather-mist cologne an the whisky spritzzers in a meenit.

Here we gang! Oan yer richt, thon's the Edinburry Castle as ye micht hae guessed frae the gey fortified luik o it. Aye they stanes are fair soaked in History!

Ablow it, Princes Street gairdens, the only public park in the world wi a railway station in it an a chip-shoap wi a patio. Haunds up fur fish suppers!

103

Noo mind an tak a guid luke at the erchitecture aw owre the place. The famous Scottish poet, Ian MacRae, compared it tae a muckle cash-register, wi aa the shoaps in Princes Street springin up.

Ahint the Castle, oan a braw bricht moonlicht nicht like the nicht, ye can make oot the Scottish Tourist Bureau's latest hologram shrooded in gloomy mist special effects tae gie youz ignorant foreigners the idea it's gey auld. Aye, Ah'm talkin aboot Arthur's Seat an the famous Salisbury Crags. An tae yer left, doon Dundas Street, the Firth o Forth an Fife.

Yon's The Scottish National Ert Gellery fair bustin at the seams wi maisterpieces frae aa owre the world. The Scottish yins? They're in the archives. Afore it's the R.S.A. or Republican Scottish Army H.Q. Thon used tae be an ert gellery anaa. Notice the steps up tae the National are a sicht mair worn doon than the steps up tae this yin – that's cause it's free!

Oan yer richt, Waverley Station! Richt that's aa yez need tae ken! Off yez gawn! Next load oan! Nae shovin!

The tour-guide burbled uncontrollably through his head as the bus jerked and lunged its way from one set of lights to another. Outside, shops were beginning to shut and queues were forming at bus stops. Everybody looked huddled and cold and miserable.

He wiped away the condensation on the window and peered out as the bus swung into Leith Walk and plunged headlong between the darkening tenements.

All the best sinners hurry down to hell
Or Leith, or the Cowgate,

It was a line of MacRae's. He must phone him up and see what he was doing for It. And Grogan. And Yvonne. Christ, it was the last day of the year, she wouldn't be able to deny him. They had to meet, it was ordained. Everybody would meet in a pub. Choosing the right one would be difficult. It always was. They would all be packed to the gills and they would all shut too early, leaving too long a time before the bells. There would be the goodbyes, the confusion of who was

104

going where with who else, people would miss each other and catch up with each other after, and so on into the night, up to the bells.

Where to be at the bells? There was the party at Tony McTaggart's. The Out-crowd would no doubt be there in force. Then there would be the party at the Producer's place, where *The Hogmanay Show* would certainly be showing. That would be one to take Yvonne to, if she would go. Maybe she'd be impressed despite herself by his apparition on t.v. Anywhere but the Tron.

The possibilities of the night ahead began to suggest themselves, but he would think about his options later, or maybe he wouldn't have to. Maybe the New Year would take over, as it often did, and carry him along with its momentum. First, Semple. He counted his money. It wasn't enough.

The thing is, Mr Semple, I'm expecting a cheque any day from Scottish Television and when it comes, I won't even cash it, I'll sign it over to you and deliver it personally on a ceremonial maroon velvet cushion with gold tassels. It will more than cover your arrears. Look upon the extra hundred as your rightful interest.

Oh Christ Almighty.

George, you're a man of the world so I won't beat about the bush, I'll be straight with you. I may look like a dejected reject of the eighties with dim prospects for the nineties, but I have planted my seed, George, and it will flourish into a fruitful career in the growing field of Personal Security. Security Consciousness, George, that's what the nineties will bring to all of us, and I'm not talking about folk insuring their spare set of dentures against accidental loss or damage. No, George, we're talking about survival, survival in the face of the tidal wave of crime about to sweep over the streets of Edinburgh and every other city in the land.

That's where you come in, George. I'll need a few thousand lads from your private army to do a bit of door-to-door visiting. If a few of them are policemen, so much the better. Call it Operation Spyhole.

The government? Don't worry about the government, George, this idea comes to me direct from Number Ten. Our lady at the helm is concerned about the mutinous lack of enthusiasm among her kilted brothers and sisters. She told me frankly that she would have sent in the army by now but they're already away somewhere else and won't be back for a while.

She needs us, George, to collect the Poll Tax. No Poll Tax, no vote. No vote, no National Insurance Number. No National Insurance Number, no Income Support. No Income Support, no Unemployment. I hope you get my drift, George. You can leave the paperwork to me while you and your boys collect the readies. You'll have to recruit them, train them and put them in bulletproof uniforms. I suggest a light but assertive blue. The Poll Tax Protection Squad. Protection, George. The buzz-word of the nineties.

That's why I called this meeting with you today: with my technical expertise, experience of market research and sales promotion, and your assets and experience of old wardrobes, secret ceremonies and extortion, we can join forces to form a new Corporation – you'll notice I don't say 'business', George, we're not talking about the Enterprise Scheme now – no, a *corporation*, George, the word lets the world know we're doing it a service. The National Security and Protection Corporation of Scotland, George, how does that sound? Don't you agree it has a ring of authority about it?

I'll take charge of the advertising campaign. Safe as Houses, that will be our slogan, and all our houses will be safe, George – close-circuit television, armed guards, electronic moats, the works. They're already doing it in the States, and we're going to bring it to Scotland. The haves must be protected from the have-nots and we will make sure that they pay for the privelege. As for the riff-raff, we'll launch a scheme to eradicate homelessness: compulsory housing, George. The goverment will buy it, it's already been floated in The House. Imagine, George, a system of patrolled warrens under Edinburgh, each cell fitted with a metal bed screwed to the floor and a simulated view of Arthur's Seat. We'll pack them in there like sardines and pick up the housing development grants and the rent payments from the housing department as well as the design awards. You and me, George, together we will transform chaos into order: everyone locked out or locked in. We will build the best-designed prison in the history of mankind, and we will call it Scotland. Get a spare set of keys cut at the heel-bar no problem.

106

McCoy took some of the money – it was the last day of the year, he needed to keep some for his bottle and a few drinks – and put it in his inside pocket. The remainder was meagre, but it was something to offer Semple. And he could tell him he'd be moving out soon.

Yvonne, before you tell me if you are or if you aren't, Jinx and I have discussed it and we've reached a decision. We want to move in.

Please.

SEMPLE'S SECOND-HAND FURNITURE EMPORIUM had just closed up for the night as McCoy reached the door, but there was a light on somewhere inside. McCoy banged on the door and waited. The door was unlocked by a stocky figure who told him gruffly that they were shut. McCoy squinted at the man's face but the features were in shadow.

'I've come to pay a debt.'

The figure stepped aside and nodded him in. In the dim interior of the warehouse there was just enough light for McCoy to make out the scar on the man's cheek and to recognise him as the Wholesaler who had sold him the holes. McCoy averted his own face in the hope that he wouldn't be recognised and changed his voice to say: 'Yes, ah . . . Is Mr Semple available?'

'Office. Up there,' said the Wholesaler, pointing to a door with a lit window in it at the back of the warehouse. As McCoy picked his way between the wardrobes and the setees to get there, followed by the Wholesaler, he thought he heard a brief grunt of laughter behind him. When he reached the door, he was about to knock when the man's voice came close to his ear, making him jump:

'In ye go.'

George Semple stood behind the oversized metal desk in his office, browsing through *The Collector*. In his grey hair there were dyed streaks of black. His black leather jacket creaked as he moved to and fro with the air of a man who is used to working out of doors. Behind him, on the mantlepiece, was a hot-water urn, a packet of sugar, a tin of dried milk and a box of tea-bags. In one corner, partially blocking a small barred window with frosted glass, stood an ancient wooden

108

filing cabinet with a drawer missing, above which hung a girlie calendar. In another stood a standard lamp without a shade and an intricately carved oak sideboard. The floor was uneven, being layered with several overlapping carpets all with different patterns, and McCoy stumbled as he went in, followed by the Wholesaler. Semple looked him up and down and turned a page of *The Collector*.

'Eh . . . it's about my rent,' said McCoy.

Semple looked up sharply, closed the magazine, threw it down and, resting the knuckles of both hands on the desk, leaned towards McCoy to scrutinise him more closely with his acidic green eyes.

'Aw aye, yes, so it's you, is it? Welcome home, son. Todd, it's the Prodigal Son. Go and kill the fatted calf, will you?'

McCoy glanced over his shoulder at the Wholesaler, who smiled uneasily, as if he didn't know what the joke was.

'What are you on about?' said McCoy.

'Oh, we heard you'd moved in here, that's all. Some friends of ours let us know you were giving this as your address. Funny that, I mean, seeing as how this is strictly a business premises, and then, unless I'm very much mistaken, I think you're in the studio.'

'You could call it that. I call it a shed,' said McCoy.

'Now now, c'mon now son, you know as well as me that you've got a bargain there.' said Semple, affably. 'Where else in Edinburgh could you get a place as cheap as that, fully furnished as well? Have a seat.'

McCoy sat down and blew into his hands. 'The only furniture there when I moved in was the bed,' he said, 'and I had to throw that out and get a better one at a jumble sale.'

'What was wrong with the bed that was there?'

'The springs were gone. The mattress was ripped and damp. And it was a single.'

Semple frowned and looked at him accusingly. 'Oh? And why would you need a double? Have you got somebody else in there? Another wee McCoy?'

'No such luck,' said McCoy, 'my girlfriend won't even spend the night there.'

Semple glowered at him. 'You're not supposed to sleep there, McCoy, it's not a residential property. But if you wanted a bed,

109

you should've said. I had a very nice Victorian four-poster in here the other day –' He nodded to the door into the warehouse. 'That might've suited you, although . . . You're not interested in commodes, by any chance?'

'It might be an improvement on that w.c.'

'Well now, I just so happen to have a variety of quite gorgeous commodes in my Morningside showroom. If you'd care to drop in one afternoon next week I'm sure we could fix you up with something Edwardian. Where's the money you owe me, kiddo, d'you think I've got time to shoot the breeze wi the likes of you?'

McCoy took out his miserable bundle of crumpled notes and began to sort through them with difficulty, because his fingers were numb with the cold.

'Here, allow me,' said Semple, cordially.

McCoy watched him count the notes, occasionally holding one by its dogeared corner and grimacing with disgust. As he did, McCoy glanced over his shoulder. Todd the Wholesaler was still there, with his back against the door. There was something about the face that was terrifying, apart from the scar. It was the dead look in his grey eyes, like dud lightbulbs. McCoy felt as if he was being stared at by a corpse.

When Semple had finished counting he wagged the money in his hand and said, 'Where's the rest, kiddo?'

McCoy cleared his throat and told him the long, complicated story of how his giro was late because of a computer failure in the D.H.S.S., underlining the pathos of his situation with the fact that he couldn't claim rent from them because the shed wasn't legally habitable. Semple whistled lightly as he listened, occasionally stopping to mock him with an askance look and fire a humourless laugh of scorn at him.

'Oh, it's all so horribly complicated, Mr McCoy. Now, I have no real interest in your personal life, if you have one, apart from one or two teeny weeny details. How's the door-tae-door salesman making out, eh? It's called an illicit source of income, known neither to the Inland Revenue nor the Department of Health and Social Security. Isn't that interesting, Todd?' The Wholesaler grunted in the background. 'So. And what else? A secret savings account in Tollcross co-operative? Or is it Switzerland? Nothing would surprise me, Mr McCoy.'

110

McCoy made a performance of his laughter, then shut up when Semple threw him a look so affable that it was threatening.

'We have a comedian here, Todd,' said Semple. 'In fact, I've been given to understand that he does do the odd spot in a club here and there, in a professional capacity. C'mon then, McCoy, make us laugh. Todd there hasnae had a good laugh for the last thirty years. Say something funny.'

'You're doing okay, Semple, and the nineties will be even better for you. The Poll Tax suits you all right, eh? It would've suited Rachman as well –'

Semple raised his eyebrows, as if expecting something more.

'That's not very funny, is it Todd?'

'No,' said McCoy, 'but it's true.'

Semple walked around the desk and stood in front of him. 'Ah, tell him he's not funny any more Todd, will you?'

McCoy was half-way out of the seat and beginning to turn when a broad fist blocked his view of its owner as it thumped him in the eye. He was shoved back into the chair and the Wholesaler's hands on his shoulders held him there.

'You're no funny any mair,' the voice said in his ear.

'No,' agreed McCoy. 'I'm not.'

Semple chuckled good-humouredly. 'The D.H.S.S. – they don't seem to find fraud very amusing these days, I'm afraid.'

'Are you threatening to blackmail me?'

Semple pretended to consider the question, pressing the nicotined fingertips of his hands together. Then he smiled and nodded slowly.

'Yes,' he said.

'Don't worry, you'll get your money,' said McCoy, weakly.

'You know, you're a complete waste of my time. I could be charging treble for that place. Quite frankly, Mr McCoy, I'd get more for it renting it out for band practice to an auld tramp wi a moothie.' He looked at McCoy in disgust, then the disgust turned into irritation. 'Anyway, I'd like you to vacate the premesis by, ah . . . well, how does tomorrow, sound? It's just that your house is due for demolition next Tuesday, I think it is. The march of progress, Mr McCoy. It has been pointed out to me that the present building you occupy is something of an eye-sore. I've more or less been pressurised into promising to replace it with a couple of luxury flatlets suitable for professional gentlemen in

111

the high income bracket, so I want you out, now is that quite clear?'

McCoy opened his mouth, but the fingers squeezing his shoulders told him to shut it again. He nodded.

'Splendid. Och, you've not been my worst tenant by any means. So, seeing as it's New Year and all, I'll turn a blind eye to the small matter of your outstanding arrears. Now what could be fairer than that?'

'But –' But a thump on the shoulder squashed the objection he was trying to squeeze out. Two thumbs dug into the back of his neck while Semple smiled at him affably and said: 'A little gratitude, where it's due, is never out of place, Mr McCoy.'

'Thanks! Thank you! I really appreciate . . . everything . . . very much . . . I'm really . . . grateful!'

It was difficult to get the words out because of the Wholesaler's tightening grip on his throat. When Semple nodded and the Wholesaler let him go, McCoy fell out of the chair on to the floor.

'Consider yourself evicted,' said Semple, dropping his affability for a moment. McCoy picked himself up and walked to the door. As he stepped through it into the warehouse, shadowed by the Wholesaler, he heard Semple call:

'Oh – and a Happy New Year!'

ALTHOUGH IT WAS dark and cold and wet, he didn't wait for a bus. He walked up Leith Walk, fingering the swollen area around his eye. It had started to throb painfully. He would be bringing in the New Year with a keeker. The New Year. It had never been a straightforward, happy time for him, it had always caught him at a bad time, a time of uncertainty, a time when the future looked as if it might be harder than the past. The past was hard too, but at least it was over. Or was it?

The first time he got drunk had been at New Year. In the Steamies. Just kicked out of school and the future looking bleak already. Deliberately getting as drunk as he can before going out with his pals, Archie Slater and Vincent Gray. Archie is getting drunk too, or at least making the most of acting drunk. But Vince isn't. He's sitting there on a hard chair with his legs apart, as if he's in his own house, talking to John McCoy who, his eyes blurred by the booze, is nodding and smiling at him.

The youth McCoy resents the way Vincent Gray and his old man are getting along like a house on fire. Vincent has been saying the right things and his father is by turns beaming at Vincent and glowering at him and Archie.

'Hear that? That's mair like it. That's what a boy your age should be like. No a flamin sufferin jessie like you!'

The youth McCoy flicks back his shoulder-length hair, makes a jeering noise and upturns what must be his fourth can of export.

'Time for a song,' says his father, taking the floor and holding his glass out in front of his face as if it's a microphone. 'When Irish eyes are smiling –'

His older sister Frances is there, giving him disapproving looks every time he puts the can to his lips. His sister Mary and her new

113

boyfriend Richard are there on the couch, looking bored. They are looking at him disapprovingly as well. The youth McCoy hiccups stupidly and Archie Slater rolls his eyes at him and nods to the door. It's the first year they've been let out, allowed to leave their own houses and go to the town clock and then on to a party. They're determined to make the most of it.

When his father's Irish eyes have stopped smiling, Richard clears his throat to sing. He's still got his arm round Mary as he starts to sing, but as soon as he starts, Frances jumps out of her seat and slaps him hard across the face.

'How dare you sing that filth!'

'Aye, none of that here!' shouts John McCoy, though he looks vaguely bewildered at finding out that his older daughter has stepped into the fray before he's had the chance to himself. His power is beginning to slip.

Mr and Mrs Schmidt, who have been behaving themselves like good German neighbours until now, add to the tension by asking what this song is and what is wrong with it.

'The Dundee Weaver by Christ!' shouts John McCoy, rousing his indignation and stabbing at the air with his finger. 'Ye should be ashamed o yersel!'

The boyfriend begins to look sheepish as the commotion he's caused looks as if it might get out of hand.

Enter his mother, with a plate stacked high with sandwiches.

She seems blissfully unaware of the bad feeling in the room, and as if to protect her innocence, everyone pretends that nothing has happened.

'What about Pat? Is he no gawnae dae a turn?'

It's his cue to get the hell away. He nods meaningfully to his mates and they back him up against all the exhortations to stay for the bells. It's been arranged. They're all meeting at the steeple.

Pauline. That's where he'd met Pauline. And they'd spent the night together, on the couch in somebody's house, necking and fondling under cover of a coat, because some old woman was there who wouldn't go away. The old bag had sat there on a chair all night to make sure nothing could happen . . .

Now here it was again, but without the family. It was desperate. It was hellish. The only thing to do was to get pissed and go through with it all again. He would wake up tomorrow hungover but cleansed.

Or maybe he should make this New Year the one New Year when he stayed in and stayed sober, but the thought of spending it alone in the shed filled him with dread.

On the other hand, he didn't have the shed for much longer. One more night, to be exact. He could light a fire in the stove. He could listen to the radio. A cosy little picture began to paint itself in his mind: there he sat in his tattered old armchair, his feet toasting in front of the stove, a hot toddy by his elbow, Jinx on his lap, reading Dickens and listening to Mozart until *The Hogmanay Show* came on. He could wish his black-and-white t.v. ghost a happy New Year and hold Jinx's paws as he sang *Auld Lang Syne*. Or perhaps a little creative work, nothing too strenuous, work out a new stage routine . . . or maybe the writing of a letter, with brown ink, on good paper . . . Dear Mr Semple, May I begin by wishing you and your family a very good New Year and my sincere best wishes that it will bring you all you strive for. Thank you for being so understanding and magnanimous in the matter of my rent arrears. You will be pleased to hear that since our interview this afternoon I have secured several properties in the New Town area and I wondered if you could recommend suitable tenants . . .

He turned off the Walk into Union Street and headed back to the shed. He had to get himself organised. A wash, a shave and a change of clothes would be the thing. He could start at the Dundas Arms. Phone a few people from there.

Here it comes. Here comes the night.

The dansette in Loanhead Youth Club went on thumping it out inside him as he headed along London Street.

115

SOMETHING HAD DRAWN her here, but now that she stood outside the door in the wall that led down to the shed, she didn't know what to do. She knocked on the knocker, half-heartedly. Why had she come? The same need for confirmation that had taken her along the Water of Leith to the Dean Bridge? She knew it as a fact, but it hadn't come home to her, she didn't know what it meant. And his reason for doing it – maybe a clue could be found in the shed.

She was determined to find a way in. It was a challenge and she had always liked challenges. Wasn't that why she was a teacher, and in the school she was in? Wasn't that also what had drawn her to Pat McCoy in the first place? He was a challenge.

But finding a way into the shed was a different kind of challenge, the kind she hadn't dealt with for years. A physical challenge. It reminded her of being a girl.

She lit a cigarette although it hurt when she smoked. If only the icicle inside her would thaw, but it was as sharp as ever, a cold stabbing pain that shot through her back into her chest. She threw away the cigarette before it was finished and walked away from the door.

Along the wall from the door, there was another door which led to a narrow piece of wasteground which seemed to run along behind the drying greens. Using an old milk-crate to stand on, she hoisted herself on to the back wall. It was a long drop into McCoy's garden, but not so far to the sloping, corrugated roof of the shed. She eased herself down to it carefully. The sheets of corrugated iron were iced over, but above the ice the bolts that held the thing together stood up, and she used these as handholds as she slithered down the sloping roof to the front

116

of the shed. Here, she had to dreep down on to the rickety wooden staircase in front of the shed door. She fell clumsily – she hadn't dreeped for years – but caught hold of a wooden support to stop herself tumbling backwards down the stairs. Then she heard Jinx miaowing behind the door and felt more determined than ever to gain access.

She had never broken in anywhere before, but had once called on the services of a policeman to kick open her own door when she had locked herself out. His technique had been to repeatedly ram the door with the sole of his boot.

It didn't work.

She went down the stairs into the garden and walked around the side of the shed. She climbed up on the brick foundation and edged her way along the shed wall to a window. It was unlocked. When she pushed it she almost lost her balance as it flew open, her elbow bursting one of the panes.

She climbed in, hampered by Jinx, who sprang on to the windowsill and started miaowing with desperate gratitude and rubbing up against her legs.

She lowered herself into the shed, found the light switch and surveyed the wreckage of his living quarters, the catastrophe of the bed, the mess of clothes and books and plates and cups everywhere.

It was awful.

The cat was starving. It was going wild around her ankles. She kept tripping over it as she looked around. There was no note, nothing. She opened the door in the shed and went down to the cellar-kitchen. Jinx followed her, miaowing all the way. The kitchen was freezing cold and when she thought she heard something moving behind the bread bin, she hurried out and couldn't face going back into the shed again.

What to do about the cat?

She couldn't just leave it. She picked it up and wrapped her coat around it, so that only its head could be seen sticking out between the buttons. The beast started miaowing desperately. She'd get a taxi if she could see one.

HE STAGGERED DOWN the stairs to the door of the shed but stopped when he saw that it was open. The light was on.

He entered cautiously, half expecting Semple and the Wholesaler to be waiting for him. They weren't, but something had disturbed the congealed silence, the heavy smell of stale loneliness. The mess had been rearranged. There was broken glass on the floor.

He crunched over it to the window and saw that it had been forced.

The laughter in his head that wouldn't go away eddied its way out in a shaking spasm followed by a thin, high-pitched whinge that sounded like pain and surprise chasing each other up a staircase. It shook him, it rattled him, it brought tears to his eyes as he reeled around the room, out the door and down the stairs, into the subterranean kitchen with the rats. How could he have lived here, cooked his meals here?

It was so inconceivable it made him laugh all the more as he ran back up the stairs to the lesser hell of the shed, where he paced up and down, laughing wildly as he tipped a shelf of books to the floor and couped a chair. He saw a cup sitting on the floor and he kicked it against the stove, where it smashed to pieces.

The sound it made as it shattered interrupted the laughter for a second, then the laughter continued, changing all the time. One minute it was a forced and mirthless laugh full of anger and anguish, the next it was the controlled chuckle of amusement of someone laughing on cue. In another minute, it had swelled to fill the hollow silence of the room with its furious shouts.

That his pitiful dump of a home could have been thought worthy of breaking into was laughable, but he wasn't laughing

118

about that any more. He wasn't laughing about anything any more. He was sobbing out great gouts of black laughter at nothing. He sank to his knees in front of the stove and went on until the laughter had exhausted itself.

Where the hell was Jinx? A cat burglar.

False laughter. A groan.

Maybe the cat had broken out? Could a cat force a window? He wouldn't put it past Jinx. She was a survivor, and the windows weren't what you could call catproof.

Had anything been taken? No! There was nothing worth taking! The burglar had taken one look and got the hell out.

He should do the same.

He had to see Yvonne. It was a dramatic entrance, if not exactly the most welcome one. Yvonne, my home has been ransacked, my most treasured possession stolen. A cat. Open your heart to a victim of brute circumstance and make me a cup of tea and maybe some of that Portuguese stew with the cabbage and the hot sausage, something to sustain a man in times of desperation, in times of great sorrow on the last day of the year. Yvonne, look at me, look into my eyes, and if you can't forgive me for whatever I said –

You can't even remember what you said, you were so pissed . . .

That's what she'd say. Something like that. But then he'd concede the point:

I was so pissed, Yvonne, I didn't know what I was saying. It wasn't me saying it, it was the drink talking. I was feeling disappointed in myself, depressed about the world in general and anxious about my future in it.

That just about covered everything.

He stopped pacing and stood still, struck by the similarity between what he was saying in his mind to her and the way he talked to an audience. The best survivors knew how to use their vulnerabilities, they didn't need a spy-hole, they had a hole in the door anyone could get a crowbar through.

What did he want? To be taken back out of pity?

Okay, he wouldn't mention the break-in, in case she thought he was playing for sympathy.

No, he'd clean himself up, get a bunch of flowers at the late-night grocery and do a Richard Burton in *Who's Afraid of*

Virginia Woolf there on her doorstep, the bit where he appears on the doorstep with the flowers for Liz Taylor and imitates a tongue-tied country boy. He'd do an imitation of the imitation. It was one of her favourite films. It couldn't not work.

He needed a shave, a quick wash with a kettle of water, a change of clothes. Something to go better with the imitation brogues than what he was wearing. There must be something worth keeping, something worth salvaging of his life to date. Wasn't there anything? The electric fire might come in handy. The radio. The black and white t.v. His dribs and drabs of clothes. A few dog-eared books. He could come back for them in the morning. No! There was nothing worth keeping, it was all junk, none of it mattered. None of it was working. None of it was any use at all.

Jinx was right. Get out before the going gets worse.

He ran down to the kitchen, filled the kettle and set it on the cooker.

He needed to eat something. The corned beef roll in his coat pocket. That would do. He needed a drink. It had been a bad day, all right, all the more reason to make it a good night. Night was here. This was it. New Year. He had to get to the Dundas. He had to phone everybody.

PEOPLE WERE GIVING her strange looks as she hurried through the slush with the cat's head peeping out of her coat, but she didn't care. She felt as if she had achieved something by capturing it.

A car blared its horn at her and the cat tried to bolt out of her coat, but she held it. She hurried on to her close and slammed the door behind her. She put the cat down and leaned against the door. The cat immediately began to size up the close, sniffing around corners, miaowing urgently and looking at her as if to say, What now?

She had no trouble persuading it to follow her upstairs and into her flat. Once inside, it became even more agitated, and kept rubbing its matted pelt against her legs and miaowing urgently and looking at her with begging eyes.

Was this what was left of him? A starved orphan of an animal who greeted her every attention with a look of such pathetic gratitude that she could hardly bear to look it in the eye?

When she took the tin of tuna from the cupboard, the miserable creature was up on its hind legs, pawing her knees and clawing her jeans. She pushed it away from her and rummaged in the drawer for the tin opener. There was something alarming about the cat's persistence. It kept jumping up at her as she opened the tin, rubbing against her legs and miaowing at her in a voice that was eerily human, and too much like a baby's for comfort.

When she scooped the tuna into a saucer and set it down on the floor, the beast went for it as if the wad of dead tuna meat still had to be caught. It yanked a lump of the pink meat from the saucer on to the floor and uttered a sound low in its throat that was part gloat and part growl and sounded like an animal impersonating a person. It was clear whose cat it was. The whole

121

thing was an impressive performance – pure cat, but at the same time, weirdly human. Yvonne pulled out one of the kitchen chairs and sat down to watch it as it attacked the saucer of tuna with an obscene greed she would not have believed an animal capable of. The weird thing was that everything it did seemed larger than life, not the habit of a dumb animal but the mannerism of a personality, and throughout it all there was something that smacked of Pat McCoy, though she couldn't put her finger on what it was.

Though he had consistently treated the cat with scorn the few times she had let herself be persuaded against her better judgement to go back with him to the shed, this in itself began to seem suspicious to her now. Maybe he had loved it? The thought was unwelcome. She had never been sentimental about animals and instinctively distrusted people who seemed to be capable of loving them. But then feelings of jealousy towards them were no less dubious.

And now that she thought about it, his scorn for the animal was tinged with admiration and a grudging respect. When he was drunk or in an especially good mood, he would sometimes talk about how the cat was a survivor, and would tell the story of how a couple of waifs had brought it to the door, the door of his mother's house in The Steamies. And she had taken it in and kept it for a few years. But when his father had died, she had 'cleaned the house', obliterating every trace of him. Pat had told her about it more than once, how his mother had got him to lug two black plastic bags full of his father's possessions to the old folk's home at Broomieknowe, as if the dying would welcome a gift of a dead man's things. The thought of him doing it made her shudder with more conviction now than it had when she had first heard it. And somehow the cleaning of the house had entailed putting the cat down.

And so he had taken the cat in.

The survivor looked up at her quickly, as if sizing her up. Its jaws went on doing what they were doing to the tuna. Every so often it would open them wide and lick around its mouth with a flickering tongue.

It looked like she was stuck with it for life. They would grow old together, two spinsters, two survivors, with the added curse that they were of different species and spoke different languages.

The cat looked up at her again, and this time disarmed her by stopping what it was doing for a moment and cocking its head and looking at her with curiosity. At the same moment, she got the feeling that this cat was an old rogue, a practised and cynical chancer impersonating some cute cattish antics with heavy irony because it had learned that this was what was required of a cat in the human world. But although its tongue went on flickering around its mouth, it seemed to have lost interest in the food for a minute.

Then it was wolfing its way into the remains of the tuna, until it had licked the plate clean. The elaborate ablutions followed.

She decided to have a bath as well. Change her clothes. Put her make up on. Go out and get drunk. It was the last day of the year, after all. It was another course of action, and that was what she needed. And she needed to feel warm. The icicle inside her was brittle, jagged. If it snapped it would wound her. She had to thaw it out gradually. It could take years, it could take the rest of her life.

A LEAN ALSATION prowled around the door to the Dundas Arms. Leashed to a nearby lamp-post, it panted back and forward on the muddied threshold.

As McCoy approached, it stopped, both ears cocked, and tasted the air between them. He could see its nostrils working as it uttered a ferocious growl.

'Good doggy.'

It berated him in a tirade of rabid barks.

'Nice doggy.'

He impersonated the clicking noise people make when they address dogs, but it cut no ice with this one.

It started pacing up and down more rapidly, its long tongue lolling out wolfishly, back and forward on the muddied snow, barking as if to gobble up the steam of its own panted breath.

McCoy took a step forward.

'Good doggy.'

It lunged at him, pulling the leash taut. He made the clicking noise again, but this only infuriated the beast further. It lunged at him again and bared its jagged jaws. The leash slipped down the lamp-post a few inches. He brought the uneaten remnant of his lunch, the flattened and congealed corned beef roll, from his pocket, tore a piece of it off, held it up and wiggled it.

'Here doggy.'

It rolled its tongue around its jaws, drooling long slavers of dripping mucus and voicing a canine whine. McCoy threw the scrap of meat, if it was meat, and made a run for the door as the dog went for it. It caught the offering before it hit the ground and bounded back for more. Its serrated jaws tore the rest of the roll from his hand as he burst through the door.

124

It was an entrance.

The barman bawled at him: 'Whit's the gemm? That door wis there afore you were born, an it'll be there efter ye're deid!'

The old men looked up from their dominoes and one or two shook their heads. One or two of the younger men standing at the bar looked over their shoulders at him grimly.

McCoy walked importantly to the bar.

'That dog out there! It went for me! Just about took my hand off!'

The barman scowled at him.

McCoy ordered a pint and a whisky. The man standing next to him at the bar turned to stare at him. The slicked-back hair. The imitation leather jacket. The open-necked shirt in December, printed with the kind of pattern that used to be found on drinking tumblers – made up of circles, squares, triangles and intersecting lines.

McCoy appealed to him with a shrug of the shoulders, a nod of the head, a widening of the eyes and a turning outwards of the open hands – a mime show designed to demonstrate his own honesty and innocence in all matters. The man went on staring at him steadily.

'I'm telling you,' said McCoy. 'It's wild. No wonder the pub's half empty – nobody can get in the door!'

'That's ma dug ye're talkin aboot, friend.'

He saw the hook where the man's hand should be and felt the eyes harden on his. The left one had stopped throbbing on the way back up from Leith, but now it was beginning to swell.

'Is it really? It's a big animal. Must cost you a bit to feed.'

He hoped this would smooth things out, but it only seemed to add offence to injury. McCoy, feeling the smile congeal on his face, paid for his drinks and retreated to a corner of the pub, next to the fruit machine. He sat down and tasted the beer – it tasted rich and bitter, a sour nourishment. It made him shudder with pleasure. He gulped some more, then sipped at the whisky. He felt it go all the way down, a river of fire inside him.

He fingered his eye gingerly. It was swelling fast. Soon it would darken.

He counted the money he had left after his visit to Semple. It wasn't enough to go on drinking *and* buy his bottle. There was a

125

choice involved that was really no choice at all. The worst kind to make.

But I'd decided I wanted to live with you *before* I was evicted, Yvonne, honest.

If she was pregnant, though, it would be hard to make the choice that was no choice at all and move in. If she still wanted him to. Maybe she'd look at him through her spyhole – oh yes, he'd done one for her in the first flush of his enthusiasm – and not open the door.

Don't look at me through your spyhole, Yvonne. At least open the door.

He realised that he'd left his haversack in Semple's office.

To hell with the damned malicious things, they should never have been invented. To see but not be seen. It wasn't a position of defence. It was a position of attack.

This hole-selling caper was not for him. He was cut out for other niches. He would look into window-cleaning the moment the new year got off the ground. All he would need would be a chamois, a good chamois and a bucket. The ladder and the van – he'd need a van eventually of course – could wait until he was well established.

Suddenly, he was struck by a thought so simple, clear and beautiful that he felt like telling it to someone immediately: there were more windows than doors. Of course there were. And you could do them again and again, the same streets, the same houses, the same windows . . .

Good morning Mrs Grainger, it's me again, your window-cleaner with a smile and a chamois over my shoulder. What's that Mrs Grainger, you're surprised to see me again so soon? You thought I'd done them only last week? But I keep a record in my little book Mrs Grainger and from this it's quite clear that your windows have not been washed for a full month – nay, more than a month, a good five weeks of the city's grimes dim your elegant panes, and the astonishing views they afford – the Firth of Forth at the back, the Pentland Hills to the front and Edinburgh Castle from the Master Bedroom window. A coffee-morning, Mrs Grainger? And which is the lucky charity this week, if I may be so impertinent to enquire? Homeless cats? Yes indeed, I myself have given shelter to just such an unfortunate creature Mrs Grainger, on a temporary basis until I find her a good home. If you could see your way to making a few enquiries on my behalf, I would be eternally grovelling. She is clean, cute and house-trained. I would be no trouble either – a cupboard under the stairs and a humble mattress upon the floor would fulfil my wildest dreams. You might install a small bell, Mrs Grainger, with which to summon me every time your windows require cleaning. Rest assured I will on no account distract you ladies from your noble colloquy. Proceed as if I were not there. No Mrs Grainger, thank you, I will not have coffee, for I carry a flask which I leave in my humble van, of which I will partake with relish when my morning's work is done. It's not a wonderful job, I know, but skilled in its way and I hope you'll agree necessary. I'll be in and out in a jiffy and if you permit me, whistle a little, exchange a cheerful smile with you and your guests and make your windows resplendent, if you would just be so good as to provide me with some ordinary cold water, Lady Grainger, and a newspaper – would it be *The Telegraph* or *The Scotsman*? It doesn't matter which, it's the print that brings up the sparkle on the glass, as my father and his father before him often told me, for I hail from a long line of window-cleaners, Lady Grainger – I entered the trade at birth. Yes, it's in my bones.

The beauty of it was that all he needed was a chamois, a chamois and a bucket. Yvonne might have those items. He should give her a ring anyway.

Yvonne, listen, I'm really sorry. I love you and I regret whatever it was –

Too much of a condolence.

Hi, Yvonne! Sorry about that night. I was drunk. Listen, I'm in the Dundas Arms –

She'd hang up.

Yvonne, listen, you don't happen to have a chamois, do you?

Maybe he'd phone her later.

The whisky spread its slow fire along his veins. The beer lumbered along after it. He went to the bar for another nip. He saw his eye in the mirror behind the bar. It was going to be bad. He shut his eyes to avoid looking round the place, feeling like the kid who tries to hide by covering his eyes. He heard it all with his ears anyway: the beer skooshing from the tap into the glasses, the hoarse life-history going on on his left, the talk about the Hearts and Hibs game on his right, the coughs and grunts of the old men and the clack of their dominoes.

He opened his eyes and saw Tony McTaggart at the other side of the bar. He smiled over to him and raised a hand in greeting.

Tony McTaggart froze, his pint half-way to his mouth, seeing him but apparently not recognising him. McCoy nodded vigorously and raised his pint, but Tony went on staring at him in horror. McCoy did a little mime-routine, pointing to his swollen eye and grimacing, hoping to bring a smile of recognition to Tony's face. When it didn't, McCoy felt the queasy feeling sweep over him. It was the Overcoat Feeling again. Like being tried on by somebody else. The third time today it had happened. It was definitely getting beyond a joke. It was like an illness. Maybe it was an illness. To be somebody, somebody else, somebody not –

He tried to shout above the noise of the bar that he would see him at the party, but McTaggart looked like somebody looking out of a photograph – one he didn't know he was in. Then he shook his head, as if to bring himself out of a trance, drained his glass in a hurry and marched out of the pub.

Like those pictures the girl in the box-room had talked about, people's reactions to the sight of him were beginning to give him the message: that he was *persona non grata* – the mere sight of him made them want to flee.

Christ, it can't be that bad.

First Jan Pringle, now Tony McTaggart. Something was definitely not right. Maybe it was because it was the last day of the year. People did strange things. Sometimes people went missing and surfaced a few days later in Portsmouth.

Maggie Jordan. Going out with Tony. So he would see her at the party, if he got there. She was the common factor.

He wondered what the fuck she had been saying about him.

He made the whisky a double. Fuck it, it was the last day of the year, he was just getting a head-start on some of the others. The others? Where were the others? Time was getting on – soon the year would be over and he for one wouldn't be sorry to see the back of it. On the other hand, it meant another year had passed, another year of his life on the planet Earth and what did he have to show for it? Nothing, if that. Still, it had to be celebrated and it had to be mourned. The year's wake was a terrible celebration,

128

but it had to be attended to with due gravity. He had to make contact with somebody soon.

He decided to phone his mother.

The phone was down a narrow flight of stairs which also led to the toilets. He dialled the number and when the pips went, put in a ten pence.

'Hello Mum.'

'Is that you, Michael?'

'No, it's Patrick.'

'I'm expectin Michael to phone from Crawley. Hello, son. Are you in Edinburgh?'

'Aye, Mum. How are you?'

'Well, I've just wallpapered the hall but I've got a bad pain in my back. I think it's the weather, is it raining there?'

'You shouldn't be wallpapering at your age, Mum.'

'Have you got a job yet, son?'

'No.'

'Aw. Are you coming hame, son?'

'I will soon, Mum.'

'Aw, I though you might come hame. I'll be waitin up to watch you on the telly. I'll tell Michael, when he phones. Only, he doesn't get STV down there.'

'Wish him a happy New Year from me, eh?'

'Okay, son. Well, cheerio then, mind and dress warm and don't get into any trouble now –'

'Wait a minute, Mum, I want to talk to you.'

'How, what's wrong, son?'

'Nothing's wrong, Mum, I just want to talk to you. It's the last day of the year. I'd come home, but, well . . . you'll not be staying up late, will you?'

'Not since your faither died, son, I like to get my sleep.'

'Will Mrs Payne not be coming down?'

'Naw, she's got her laddies hame.'

'Why don't you go up to hers, Mum?'

'Aw, naw, I'll just stay where I am son.'

'You could go and first-foot the Schmidts though.'

She sniffed non-committally into the phone.

'Leave the wallpapering till I come, Mum, I'll finish it off for you.'

'It'll get done.'

Then the pips went and they said cheerio and happy new year until they were cut off. He went back up the stairs and sat down. He had phoned his mother, but what good had it done him? She had thought he was his elder brother. And he had forgotten to thank her for the Christmas tenner, forgotten to apologise for not sending her a card. Still, at least he'd called.

He looked around the bar. A drunk man was playing the one-armed bandit next to his table.

'Awright, son?'

McCoy shrugged and nodded. The man stopped playing the bandit and stared at him with a look of incomprehension. Everything was askew about him – the crumpled khaki raincoat, the trilby tilted over one eye, the shirt collar sticking up at one side, the way he was swaying and holding on to the one-armed bandit, bringing a crushed cigarette to his lips, which shut around it like a squint vice. Even his face seemed to be leaning over to one side, as if he had always looked at the world side-on.

He turned his attention back to the one-armed bandit.

'Bastard,' he said to it.

McCoy watched him playing the machine. There was nothing unusual about a drunk man playing a one-armed bandit, but there was something obsessive about the way this one was dropping coin after coin into the slot, each time uttering a gruff curse as he wrenched the handle, then waiting in silence as the bells and bars and clusters of grapes spun and juddered into line.

If he won, he would immediately feed another coin into the slot and wrench the handle – even before stooping to collect his winnings. When he lost, he would remonstrate violently with the machine before going on, shaking it from side to side between his big hands and thumping the flashing, bleeping structure with the side of his fist, shouting: 'Christalmighty, gi'us a chance!'

It was the moment of the man's waiting McCoy found himself watching, because it was then, while the symbols whirred before his eyes, that he seemed to become completely oblivious to everything. His eyes took on a dreamy kind of look, his fist relaxed its grip on the handle and his mouth hung open. McCoy wanted that too, he needed that too, that moment of oblivion. Sometimes the drunk man would interrupt that moment of waiting to shout: 'For Christsake, gi'us a hold!'

130

Then he would relax again and the faraway look would come into his eyes as he waited for the symbols to thud into line. He went on and on like that as McCoy watched, sometimes winning, usually losing, cursing and remonstrating with the machine and having his moments of oblivion.

What was he cursing and remonstrating with, apart from the one-armed bandit? What he was letting go of when his fist loosed its grip on the handle and his eyes took on the faraway look?

Sometimes his moment of oblivion would outlast the motions of the machine, so that the symbols would thud into line before his eyes but he wouldn't see them, being given over to waiting. He seemed to look beyond the line of dollar signs, plums and gold bars into the void. At such times he'd sometimes miss a hold, then reprimand himself: 'For fucksake, get a grip!'

After a while he sagged to his knees and searched in the pay-out tray. He came up with a solitary coin held aloft between finger and thumb. He swayed against the bandit and regained a kind of balanced imbalance. He looked over to McCoy again, nodded and held the coin out at arm's length, as if he was a magician holding something out for the audience's inspection.

Against his will, McCoy had become the audience. Everyone else in the bar was ignoring the drunk old bastard. Now he wanted some audience participation. McCoy took the ten pence from him, examined it, nodded to show that he was satisfied that it was genuine, then handed it back to him. Now he was going into mime-show. He put the coin between his teeth and bit on it, then indicated the bandit with a sweeping gesture of his hand. He uttered a few explanatory sounds, not quite words, then took up his position in front of the bandit, holding the coin at the slot but not putting it in yet.

'Drumroll!' he growled at McCoy.

McCoy nodded to him and smiled. One or two of the regulars were giving him looks. Christ, he had to get out of here.

'Drumroll!' shouted the drunk man.

McCoy obliged, drumming his fingers on the table. The drunk man tried to fit the coin into the slot of the bandit, but it slipped from his fingers and bounced off the machine. He wheeled around wildly as he tried to trap the rolling coin underfoot, veering towards the door and collapsing sideways. Everyone in the bar turned to watch as the drunk man hit the floor noisily.

131

The barman came around the bar, throwing McCoy a dark look as he passed his table, and walked over to where the drunk man was lying. He stood over the casualty and, watched by everyone in the bar, clasped his hands in prayer, intoned a latinate mutter and genuflected briefly. One or two of the men at the bar laughed and applauded. Feeling somehow responsible for the drunk man, McCoy went over to help the barman haul him to his feet. They walked him over the floor and leaned him up against the one-armed bandit. The barman shook him.

'Have you no got a hame tae go tae?' said the barman.

'Naw!' roared the drunk man, and his face became a tight, fierce mask.

'It's time ye were goin there anyway,' said the barman, poking him in the chest repeatedly.

'Is he not a regular?' McCoy chimed in, but the barman ignored him and went on warning the drunk man: 'Any more bother and you're out that door.' He poked his finger into the drunk man's chest with every word.

Something seemed to click in the drunk man's mind and his fierce mask dropped to reveal the face of a demoralised drunk. Now he went into an elaborate routine of apologising. His head began to nod slowly and his whole body sagged as he held up a pacifying hand and said sorry over and over again to the barman. And suddenly McCoy felt very sorry for the drunk man: wasn't he just like everyone else, except that he was drunker? Like everyone else, he wanted to be loved by the world, wanted an audience, wanted to be somebody, somebody else, somebody not himself.

The barman eased his grip on his arm.

'He's not himself,' McCoy said to the barman, who looked at him askance, 'he'll be okay.' He patted the drunk man's shoulder. 'You'll be okay, eh?'

'Ah'm fucked,' said the drunk man, simply.

'We're all fucked,' said McCoy, hoping this might console the drunk man and make the barman dislike him less.

The barman let the drunk man go and he lurched against McCoy and grabbed hold of his arm.

'Ah'm drunk, by the way,' he said in an undertone, as if it was a secret he was entrusting him with.

'I'm a bit tipsy myself,' said McCoy.

The barman shrugged and walked away, leaving McCoy with the drunk man, who held out his clenched fist and opened it to reveal the ten pence coin.

'You go,' he said.

'Who, me? You want me to put it in?'

The drunk man nodded once, and his head didn't come back up again.

'Okay,' said McCoy, 'if it wins, the money's yours.'

'Fifty-fifty.'

'Okay.'

McCoy put the coin in and pulled the handle.

'Hold, hold,' the man moaned in his ear, 'for fucksake, gi'us a hold . . .'

The symbols thudded into line, there was a click, then nothing.

'Hard luck.'

'Bastard ye, lost ma last ten pence!'

McCoy pulled another coin from his pocket hastily and offered it to him, but he wouldn't hear of it.

'Stick yer bastardin charity! A fuckin orphan, eh? Ye think Ah'm a bastardin orphan, eh? So was Jesus Christ of fuckin Nazareth. What ye gottae say tae that, eh?'

'Nothing, but look, here, have another go –'

'Fuckin right it's nothin! Nothin fuckin left! Lost the fuckin lot!'

McCoy tried to pacify him by putting a coin in the machine. Before he could pull the handle, the man took a swing at him, missed and fell on the floor. The barman came around the bar, hauled him to his feet and rushed him through the door without a word, then he came back in hitching up his trousers and gave McCoy another black look.

McCoy pulled the handle and the machine spewed its jackpot into the tray. He scooped up the coins and crammed them into his pockets. He had a hold, so he fed in another coin and won again.

It was enough for a full-bottle and more.

To hell with you, Semple. I'm rich.

He was on the point of deciding to phone Yvonne, when the lean, stooped figure of John Grogan appeared in the doorway of the bar. As soon as he saw McCoy, Grogan froze, as if stunned by some outrageous realisation.

McCoy hailed him with a raised finger, the way he'd seen someone else greeting someone somewhere else. Grogan strode over and stood in front of him, speechless. His unkempt brown beard parted to reveal a mouth twisted in a smile, and his face wrinkled up into a puzzled expression.

'Did you come out and leave the gas on, or what?' said McCoy, but Grogan did not seem to hear him.

GROGAN TOOK A STEP back and spread his arms wide.

'Pat! It really is you!'

He drew up a chair and sat down opposite McCoy without first going to the bar – a rare thing for such a man, for whom the hair of the dog was usually a matter of some urgency – and stared at McCoy with a puzzled tilt of the head and an enquiring cocking of one eyebrow. He kept on staring at him intensely, as if considering some particularly tricky moral paradox. Either that or all this was in the nature of a dramatic build-up to a declaration of penury and the request for a loan.

'How are you, John?'

'Just out of bed. A long night last night with Camus' *Rebel*, Stevenson's *Jekyll and Hyde* and the World Service News, relieved only by an old repeat of *Hancock's Half-hour*. Now there's another case in point.'

'Another case of what?'

'Manic depression. There must be something about comedy that makes it worse than tragedy.'

McCoy nodded. 'It makes people look worse. Not worse than they are. Nothing could be worse than that.'

'Whereas your average tragedy's an altogether more ennobling affair. At least the hero has a square go with the gods, even if he always comes off worse. For the unhappy comedian, then, suicide must look attractive: how better to reject comedy and affirm some ennobling suffering?'

As if that took care of that for the moment, Grogan nodded at McCoy's empty glass. 'What are you for?'

'Just a whisky.'

Grogan nodded decisively and strode to the bar for the drinks.

135

He was wearing the misshapen black coat, the pus-yellow scarf, the brown hill-walking boots with the studs for the laces instead of eyes, the wrinkled brown corduroy trousers and the tweed neo-bunnet relic-of-the-seventies cap he had worn since McCoy had met him at a party years ago, when he was a student of Philosophy. He still was a student of philosophy, but now he needed no books to fuel his passion for discourse and could find matter for speculation in the simplest of questions, like 'How are you, John?' or 'What have you been doing?' Occasionally it bordered on lunacy.

He turned from the bar to look at McCoy with renewed astonishment. When he came back to the table, he proposed a toast:

'To the real McCoy!' He doubled up and laughed as if it hurt, attracting the tight-lipped attention of one or two of the men holding up the bar. 'The real McCoy!' he repeated, arresting his painful-looking laughter to stare again at McCoy.

'Don't you start on about that,' said McCoy, grimly, 'I've had enough of that to last me a lifetime.'

Grogan laughed again and even leaned over the table to take McCoy by the shoulders and shake him as if he were a long lost brother.

'What's so funny?' said McCoy. 'Is it this?' He pointed to his swollen eye.

Grogan leaned over the table to scrutinise the damage, nodded solicitously and enquired: 'Who gave you that?'

'One of my landlord's henchmen. I've been evicted. I'm homeless, John.'

'Is that so? Ah well, it's probably for the best. The home you had was, I imagine, worse than no home at all. Many are.'

Grogan shook his head, screwed up his nose and gave vent to a wheezing chuckle, then stopped abruptly to stare again at McCoy, as if checking to see that he was still there.

'What the hell's up with you?' said McCoy.

'Nothing,' said Grogan. 'You're here, that's the main thing. In the land of the living, Pat, eh?'

'If you could call it that,' observed McCoy, with a nod of the head to indicate their immediate surroundings.

'You could, you could!' cried Grogan.

'All right,' said McCoy, 'I'm still in the land of the living. So what?'

'So what, he says, so what! To be alive, to be here now, in the great cunt of existence –'

'Watch yer language, you, there's ladies present,' said the barman, who was busy collecting glasses from a nearby table, where two dressed-up women were about to take their seats.

'His language'll no bother us, eh no Elaine?' said the taller of the two, lifting her bright green drink to her bright red mouth and smirking.

'Nut,' said the one called Elaine. She was a short, scrawny woman with dyed black hair, suspicious green eyes and a long, straight mouth that looked permanently disgusted.

'I was quoting Beckett,' said Grogan. The barman came over, placed a high stack of empty glasses on the table between them and bent down to speak quietly but sincerely to Grogan at close quarters.

'Ah don't care if ye're quotin the holy fuckin Bible,' he said, quietly, 'cut it out.' .

Grogan was about to enter into a debate with the barman, perhaps requesting him to define his terms, when McCoy the peacemaker held up a pacifying hand and assured the barman that they were all right, that all they wanted was a quiet drink, and that it was after all the last day of the year. The barman gave him a grudging nod before moving away with a stack of empty glasses.

'Ach,' said Grogan, loudly, 'people hurry to their deaths and don't stop to wonder who the fuck they are or why the fuck they're here, and yet here, in the seediest shite-hole on Edinburgh's underside, you use an innocent euphemism like –'

'Keep your voice down, John,' broke in McCoy.

'Cunt, as I was saying, and what happens? You get told off for it.'

The two women looked over at them with a kind of hostile curiosity. The one called Elaine crossed her legs and said something about McCoy and Grogan to her friend, whereupon the friend let out a hard and sustained peal of laughter before lighting her cigarette, moving around on her seat in a deliberately provocative way and throwing a challenging look at McCoy.

McCoy gave her one of his experienced smiles. She responded

137

by raising her eyebrows and rounding her eyes in a look of mock innocence. McCoy was about to repeat and develop the smile, when her friend began to talk seriously to her and she looked away.

'The real McCoy!' laughed Grogan.

'Stop it!' said McCoy, testily. 'You know I hate my name!'

'But why do you hate it?'

'You tell me.'

'Because it's yours and because it's not yours – as well as being your surname, the "McCoy" has found a place in everyday usage, viz. in the expression "the real McCoy".'

McCoy nodded.

'You resent the way your name has become associated with the expression in the minds of all those who hear it. In short, you hate your name because it has become a joke.'

'That's exactly it,' said McCoy.

'You should work out a routine about it. Use your handicaps, make the most of them –'

'That's an idea . . . . Wait a minute, that's what I've been doing all my life!'

Already he was responding to Grogan's passion for idle, speculative discourse in one of his usual ways: the Platonic disciple who merely nods, agrees with the main points propounded and answers the odd rhetorical question thrown his way by the oracle. It was a familiar routine between the two of them and McCoy didn't like it. Grogan had all the best lines. When McCoy tired of it, he would often become the devil's advocate, the heckler or, when he found Grogan's flights of logic too outrageous, the dogged and sceptical voice of common sense.

'Of course, any proper name, like any word in the language, is public property,' Grogan was saying. 'We – and it can only be self-absorption to a degree of eccentricity which allows you to delude yourself that you are the only person in the world who dislikes his name, Pat – we say we dislike our own name but in fact we're expressing the anxiety we feel about the whole inherent contradiction.'

'Eh?'

Grogan paused and smiled with real pleasure. It was one of his favourite questions from McCoy. Eh? It left the field wide open. He savoured a sip of his whisky before continuing:

138

'The contradiction inherent in our having a name at all –
something which is said to be ours, to belong to us, to be in a
sense our most personal possession, yet is at the same time an item
of public property, something which other people use to refer to
us.'

'Except in my case they use it to take the piss as well,'
complained McCoy.

'Your anxiety, in particular,' Grogan continued, 'is made
worse by the fact that your name has the added disadvantage
of being –'

'I know!' cried McCoy, with an intensity of feeling which
sounded genuine, 'I know all that, for christsake, John, I've
lived with my name! I don't want to hear about my name! I'm
desperate, John, I mean it. As my ma says, I'm at the end of my
tether. That's it, exactly. I don't know what to do.'

'About what?' said Grogan.

'About my life, and the situation with Yvonne, and now I have
to get out of the shed – everything! I've had the worst day
of my life so far, John, without a word of a lie, it started with a
terrible hangover . . .'

So McCoy related the sorry story of his day so far: the
hangover; the letter from Semple; the fight with the old man; the
police; the hole-selling; the girl in the box-room; Sandra Burnett;
buying the dead man's shoes from Willie Turnbull; going to see
Semple; the way he was strangely shunned by the teacher from
Yvonne's school and then again by Tony McTaggart – that
bit seemed to give Grogan no end of amusement – then the
drunk man playing the one-armed bandit; the phone call to his
mother . . . Grogan listened sceptically, as if at a loss to find the
thread of logic in McCoy's life.

'I think, to get to the kernel, we must first examine the causes
of these colourful effects you have described,' said Grogan,
reasonably. 'Firstly, you say that you woke up with a hangover.
Now, unless this is to be taken as an *a priori* state of affairs,
I mean that your waking automatically entails a hangover, I
think we should first ask what brought about the hangover
. . .'

'I was at a party. I got pissed. That's not the point.'

Grogan raised a nicotined, pedantic finger. 'Ah, but let us look
at it. Now, what caused you to get pissed?'

139

'It was . . . a party . . . Yvonne was there . . . we haven't been getting on . . .'

'Aha. So it's a woman. Or, by the sounds of it, a few women you have met at random during the course of the past forty-eight hours.'

'Fuck it, John, the others don't matter, I mean they do, but . . . it's Yvonne . . . I love that fucking woman . . . but I've screwed up everything . . .'

'You didn't go to the party together.' stated Grogan.

'Christ no, John, we just met there by chance.'

'Unless chance is something else,' put in Grogan hurriedly, before continuing. 'This was a party at Hugh Mitchell's place, I think?'

'How did you know that?'

'Never mind. These things get around. You'd be surprised at some of the rumours that get about.' Grogan paused here to nod meaningfully and wince with laughter. 'You say you met there by chance. So you had no idea that Yvonne would be there?'

'Well, no. I knew she probably would be. But we didn't go together.'

'But you went there, knowing that she would be there, did you not?'

McCoy could barely contain his impatience: 'Aye, okay, I knew she'd probably be there, but that's not the point –'

'So,' went on Grogan 'could we perhaps establish now whether or not there is a causal link here –'

'For fuck sake, John, it's my life you're talking about, not one of your daft wee problems of philosophy.'

Grogan paused haughtily, long enough to discount the objection before continuing: '– a causal link between your knowledge that Yvonne would probably be at the party and your going to the party?'

'Okay, okay . . . I thought she might be there. I thought if I met her there . . .'

'Was jealousy a motive?'

'For what?'

'For going. You knew it was Hugh's party. You've told me before of your suspicions, totally unfounded, in that area.'

'No, of course it fucking wasn't. Okay, I don't know. Maybe it was. So what?'

140

It felt good to be annoyed with a friend. It felt good to be getting worked up about something like this, on the other hand it was all so much nonsense the way it was coming out, the way Grogan was treating it like a subject for discussion.

'And what would you say was the substance of your falling out?'

'Shit . . .' explained McCoy, passionately, 'I miss her, John . . . I was hoping to go back to her place, honest. I remember her saying she never wanted to see me again and walking out. Because of something I'd said to her . . . I can't remember what.'

Head in hands, the penitent McCoy looked into his glass of amber whisky with an insatiable longing. His tear-ducts, normally inert, began to pulsate insistently.

'I think you said, "Tell me it's not me you don't love, Yvonne," ' said Grogan, nodding his head at each meagre monosyllable, as if reading a signpost in a language not his own. It was true. McCoy remembered saying it.

'How do you know that?' said McCoy. 'You've seen her, haven't you?'

'We spoke. On the phone. Last night.'

McCoy sat back in his chair and glared aghast at his friend.

'You spoke to her . . . last night? Why didn't you tell me?' he said, now completely beside himself. 'What else did she say?'

'She said that she would never see you again,' said Grogan, smirking conspicuously, 'and she cried a lot about it.'

'Did she say that?' said McCoy, horrified. 'But for Christsake, John, it wasn't such a terrible thing I said to her, was it? I was asking for reassurance without trying to, you know, without trying to push her into saying she still loved me, I mean what I was trying to say was –'

'Though it is hardly my place to advise you on matters of tact, for as you know my own relationships with women have been far from successful – I blame the Jesuits – I can nevertheless see exactly why Yvonne gave you the bum's rush. It was the last straw, Pat, she was exasperated beyond endurance! You're a lucky bugger, you know that. I'd give my front teeth for a woman like that.' He tugged his upper lip with a finger to show the spaces between his teeth and added, 'I've given the back yins already.'

'But I was trying to tell her –'

'I know, and she knew – she told me as much! You must

141

admit, Pat, it's a strange way to declare your love, if that is what you were trying to do.'

'I suppose it probably could have been,' said McCoy.

'You suppose it probably could have been,' said Grogan, stressing the evasive vaguenesses of McCoy's terminology.

'Well, I can't remember,' said McCoy, irritably.

'So I find that, as usual, the trouble with your life turns out to be the trouble with your woman. There's really nothing more to be said about it, or thought about it, until of course you see Yvonne later on tonight.'

'I haven't arranged to see her tonight,' said McCoy, gloomily.

'I have,' said Grogan, smugly.

'You have?'

'I said I'd drop in to see her. She's so upset, she won't even come out. But first, we'll go to meet a few people in the Café Royal.'

'I'm not going there.'

'Oh yes you are. And then you're coming to Yvonne's. She'll be delighted to see you.'

'Oh yeah. Of course she will!' said McCoy, bitterly. He caught his fleeting reflection in the window as he turned his head, noticed the way he was curling his upper lip, liked the look of it and did it again.

'Put your mind at rest, Pat, she'll be over the moon,' said Grogan, and before McCoy could dispute this further, he went on: 'We're going to pick up MacRae first. Scotland's most widely unpublished poet.'

McCoy ignored this and tried to bring the conversation back to himself: 'Anyway, you say the trouble with my life is the trouble with Yvonne, but that isn't true, John – I mean, I don't have a place to stay any more, I don't have a job –'

'These are incidentals,' maintained Grogan, 'to the main theme.'

'Which is what?' said McCoy, churlishly.

'You were saying you were desperate. Let's start again from there.'

'It's true, John, I am. I'm done in. I'm dead.'

Grogan looked at him in astonishment and said: 'Say that again.'

'What?'

142

'About being dead.'

'It's true, I'm knackered. I think I'll have an early night tonight, honestly, I don't even care if I miss the bells.'

'The bells?'

'The bells.'

'Aw, *the* bells. I thought you meant the kind that toll for thee.'

'No chance of missing them.'

After a moment's consideration, Grogan replied, 'I agree.' He went on: 'Bells or no bells, you can't get away from the New Year. Either you take part or you stay at home. Either way, you can't avoid it. So why not make the most of the celebration? But ask yourself, Pat, what is it we are celebrating when we see the old year out and the new year in? Not a natural change, not the passing of a season, because as you well know the worst is yet to come of the winter. The passage of time? Again, no. We step from the past, or before the bells, to the future, or after the bells. The bells are symbolic of the moment, the present itself. So why do we celebrate it?'

'It's quite simple,' said McCoy, 'you said it yourself – the seeing the old year out and the new year in, that's all it is.'

'Yes, but what is that, what does it mean?'

'Why ask that question?' said McCoy, the heckler in him beginning to rise to the surface, 'why not just leave it at that?'

'Questions ask themselves,' said Grogan, 'it's the answers that need our encouragement.'

'Bullshit,' said McCoy, with the right amount of belligerence.

'So why do we celebrate it?'

'Because we want to,' said McCoy.

'Need to. A hair worth splitting,' said Grogan.

'All right, need to then. Because there's nothing else to celebrate, because we're desperate.'

'Agreed. But our desperation *is* our need to celebrate.'

'Obliterate,' countered McCoy.

'Celebrate,' agreed Grogan,

'Regurgitate,' countered McCoy.

'Celebrate,' agreed Grogan.

'Masturbate,' countered McCoy.

Grogan, taking this to be a deliberate change of subject on McCoy's part, tipped his glass to his lips, drank, cleared his throat and lit a fresh cigarette from the previous dog-end.

'There is a lot to be said for masturbation. I am of course speaking from experience, the experience of my childhood confinement in a seminary run by Jesuits, during which hallo'ed soujourn I came to think of it as a secular act of genuflexion, until I was caught at it and sent to the Thrasher.'

All that was required of McCoy was to raise his eyebrows and tilt his head inquisitively, which he did.

'The Thrasher was a man employed to thrash us. When we had done something wrong, for example talking. He wasn't one of the teachers. He wasn't a janitor. His sole function was to thrash, hence his nickname. You would go through the day collecting black marks on a little blue card and then report to the Thrasher's office. There was a sink in that office. That always seemed significant to me. It taught me at an early age that the true torturer requires nothing other than what is available. Torture requires the humblest of implements. Water, for example. When the Thrasher belted you, you'd got off lightly. Water was his real weapon. The water from the tap. He held your head under it. For how long? Ten minutes? Twenty minutes? I don't know. When you are being tortured, time is subjective. Of course he had no idea what you'd done wrong and felt no particular grudge towards you. In fact, I remember him asking me how my father was doing as he held my head under the tap. He was a professional, you see. But I see this doesn't interest you in the least.'

McCoy put on a worried look.

'It's not that, John, I mean I was expelled from school, I know what you're talking about, but I'm in a bad way, I don't know if it's because it's the last day of the year or what, but today I just keep looking at my life and thinking, for fuck sake, what am I doing?'

'From your colourful account of your day, it sounds as if you're doing all right. This girl who took you in –'

'I'm not talking about her, John, I'm talking about me!' said McCoy, as heatedly as he could.

'Evidently,' said Grogan, drily.

'I mean, what do you think of me, John, I mean of my character?' said McCoy.

144

'As I think Ghandi said when asked what he thought of civilisation,' said Grogan, 'I think it would be a very good idea. What's your own opinion of your character?'

'I have none.'

'You mean the opinion or the character?'

'I think I mean . . . the opinion. Of course I do! I mean, I have a character after all, don't I?'

Grogan looked doubtful.

'So you have no opinion of your own character. Good. Neither do I, so we have common ground over which to argue.'

'I'll tell you, John, before I came out today I made my resolutions. One of them was: I shall refrain from impersonation in any shape or form. Except in a professional capacity.'

Grogan stared at him in mock horror. 'But what will you do, Pat? Take a vow of silence?'

'What d'you suggest?'

'I suggest you go abroad, where nobody knows you, and lie low for a while, then come back as a changed man and people will think: travel has changed him, or else: he feels the need to seem changed by being abroad, but really of course he's just the same old Pat McCoy we all know and distrust. On second thoughts, I suggest that you go abroad and live under an assumed name until you die. Then no one will have the opportunity to criticise you.'

'Thanks,' said McCoy, 'you're a pal. You mean no one will accept me the way I am, without the put-on voices, without the impersonations, without the act . . . But the thing is, John, something terrible's happened. I'm not funny any more.'

'Not funny?'

'I don't feel funny any more. I don't want to make folk laugh.'

'Why not?'

'Well . . . basically, it's just such a waste of my time. It's hard work, and what do I get for it? Laughter. I don't need it any more.'

'A comedian who doesn't make folk laugh. It's a contradiction in terms. It doesn't exist.'

'I do so,' maintained McCoy.

'In whose opinion?' countered Grogan.

'Mine!'

'I thought we'd already disposed of that,' said Grogan, with satisfaction. 'Anyway, if you don't exist, why should I take your opinion seriously?' Grogan laughed painfully. 'That calls for a toast. Your round.'

McCoy went to get them at the bar. He glanced over at the two women as he waited and was pleased and annoyed to see that Grogan had engaged them in conversation. He was leaning over so far that he looked in danger of falling off his chair. Whatever the story was, it was going down well. The tall one with the bright red lipstick and the green drink was laughing hard and long at every word, and even the one called Elaine with the disgusted mouth was smirking fixedly and, McCoy noticed, looking his way.

So Grogan was talking about him to the ladies. That was all right. He turned away and watched the whiskies coming his way, helped by the hairy hands of the barman, which were suddenly very clearly in focus. McCoy let himself slip into a moment of oblivion and when the barman's gruff 'Anythin else?' jolted him out of it, he felt refreshed, as if awaking from a deep and satisfying sleep. He realised his hangover had now evaporated, or at any rate had gone into hiding, from which vantage point it would ambush him at some point in the immediate future. He paid for the drinks and returned to the table in a new mood of buoyancy and acceptance: everything was as it should be, this pub, the time of night, Grogan sitting there chatting away to those two women. He could see that although they were enjoying Grogan's story they thought he was a bit weird. He was a bit weird.

McCoy wanted to keep walking to the table and never arrive there, and even hesitated in front of the one-armed bandit as if thinking about playing it again. When he sat down, Grogan was in full flight, but broke off to snatch the whisky from McCoy's hand, raise it high above his head and declare:

'Pat, meet Elaine and Janet! To the living among us!' The women looked at McCoy, then at each other, and laughed conspiratorially. 'To the living among us,' they said.

'To the living among us,' echoed McCoy.

They clinked their glasses and drank.

'And now another toast,' said Grogan.

'What's it tae be this time?' asked Janet.

'To the dead among us,' said Grogan.

Elaine and Janet went into a fit of the giggles, but Grogan looked steadily at McCoy with an expression of such gravity that

146

McCoy felt the smile fade from his own face before it had time to settle.

'What are you on about?' said McCoy.

'This is a bit morbid, is it no?' said Janet.

Elaine said: 'Aye, aw this aboot death, it's spooky. Here, there's Eddie!'

Eddie was the man with the dog and the hook for a hand McCoy had spoken to earlier. He stood at the top of the stairs to the toilet, looking over the bar. His face had set in an expression of spite, as if the very act of looking at the world was an act of combat.

He stared at McCoy as he walked slowly over to their table.

'That's ma wife ye're talkin tae!' he growled.

'Aye, worse luck,' said Janet.

'Aw c'mon now, it's New Year. See yez later, boys!' said Elaine, as she and Janet rose from their seats. 'Have a guid New Year when it comes.' Then she leaned over to tickle McCoy under his chin and say 'He's no bad lookin for a –'

But Janet slapped a hand over Elaine's mouth before she could finish. They walked away with Eddie to the other side of the bar.

'You didn't fancy mine much anyway,' said McCoy.

Grogan consulted the clock above the bar. 'Another?'

'Let's get the hell out of here, John, it's beginning to depress me.'

'Okay. Let's go and get Ian. Here. Get us a half-bottle to carry out, eh? I've got to make a phone call.' McCoy took the money, drank up and went to the bar for the half-bottle.

'Who were you phoning?' he asked Grogan when he came back up the stairs.

'Yvonne.'

'What the hell for?'

'You don't need to know,' said Grogan. 'Anyway, she was engaged. We'll try again later.'

On the way to MacRae's, McCoy handed Grogan the bottle and asked:

'Do we have to hear his poems?'

Grogan shook his head and shuddered, as if the very thought of hearing MacRae's poems made him grue.

147

THE BATHROOM WAS the worst place in the world to be. It was the loneliest place. She laid her clean clothes on the chair and turned the bath taps on. She looked at herself in the mirror above the sink. What was she doing? She was going to have a bath. She was going to get dressed. She was going to put her make-up on as if nothing had happened. She was getting herself ready to go out. Where would she go? She knew that the others had arranged to meet in the Café Royal. She knew that there was a party at Tony's place. She wouldn't go to either. Wherever she went, she would go alone. She remembered that Grogan had said he'd come round. She didn't want to see him. If he came alone it might be all right, but he'd probably bring some of the others. They would talk about the death, that's all they would talk about.

She tugged her clothes off quickly, then had to wait for the bath to fill up. A line of knickers and socks and bras hung along the shower rail. They looked shrivelled and sad. She opened the little cupboard above the sink and saw his razor and a box of blades. She took them out and looked at them. He had kept a razor there for the last year, for the mornings after the nights he stayed with her. That was the extent of the commitment. She felt angry with him for this little item of domestic foresight and threw the razor and the blades down on the shelf beside the bath.

Outside the door Jinx was miaowing to get in. She opened the door and flung a shoe at it. It sprang backwards, hissed and sat down across the hall and gave her a dirty look. She slammed the door. She turned off the taps and climbed in. She eased herself down into the water slowly. It was too hot. Or maybe she was too cold. She couldn't luxuriate in it the way she wanted to. The air was cold. When she lay down in the bath to escape it, the surface of the water cut into her breasts like a burning wire. The tap was dripping and she couldn't be bothered turning it tight to stop it.

She felt exhausted from her exertions while breaking into the shed. What good had it done her? What good was his damned cat to her? It miaowed at the door again and she threw a bottle of shampoo at it and shouted at it to get lost.

Although she'd found no clue in the shed, its emptiness had brought something home to her. He wasn't there any more. It was as simple as that. He had done it in anger, out of pure spite. He had done it to hurt her. There could be no other reason for it.

The icicle was melting, but too suddenly. It was turning into a hot river of anger running in her veins.

Suicide. The bathroom was the worst place in the world to think about suicide. She seethed, thinking about it. It was the most selfish thing anybody could do. She reached for the box of razors and took one out. She unpeeled the paper and held it between her finger and thumb. She looked at it for a long time. Then she watched her dark blood clouding the water.

A BIT OF MUSIC McCoy recognised as an advertisement from the sixties could be heard coming from MacRae's top flat as they made their way up the stairs. When Grogan paused on the stair to get his breath, he took the opportunity to say:

'Beethoven doesn't bode well. Our bard must be in the doldrums. He's been down in the mouth since his last rejection slip from the *T.L.S.*'

'Why? Is he not used to rejection by now? He said to me he was getting to like it.'

'That's what he says. Never take what a poet says at face value, Pat.' He paused, as if wondering whether to go all the way out on this limb or just look along it and point a finger.

'What he does is no different from what you do. He puts on voices. The only difference is, his voices don't make folk laugh.'

'He's sometimes funny, is he not?'

'Sometimes,' said Grogan. 'Between the poems. Or when he's not meaning to be.'

'It's like that, is it?'

Grogan shook his head. 'Not as bad as that. But this rejection slip was a bit different from all the others.'

'How?'

'Well, it wasn't the usual "The Editor Regrets That He Cannot At Present Avail Himself Of Your Work" sort of rejection slip. And it certainly wasn't the condescending, encouraging "Try again!" kind either. This guy wrote to Ian telling him never ever to submit his work again under any circumstances.'

'That's fairly clear, eh?'

'It's pretty final.'

150

There was a moment of silence when both shook their heads thinking about their rejected friend. Then they looked at each other. It was difficult to know who started first. Both were holding their breath against it. Then it came squirming out, an ugly lizard of laughter between them. They writhed with it. It wriggled inside them and spat out its flickering tongues.

When they had stopped laughing, they sank into a gloomy silence. Grogan looked up enquiringly, as if he sensed that something was amiss:

'What's up?'

'Nothing.'

'Patrick McCoy, you're a liar.'

McCoy sighed elaborately, leaned on the bannister and looked down into the dark stairwell. The music blared above them from their friend's flat.

'So it's Beethoven, is it?'

'After he went deaf, or before?' said Grogan, as much to himself as to McCoy.

'I didn't know it was Beethoven,' said McCoy.

'Oh, that's it, is it?' said Grogan impatiently. 'Feeling sorry for yourself again, because you're educationally inadequate?'

'You sound like Yvonne.' said McCoy. 'I feel like getting drunk.'

Grogan gave him a long look, then barked a cracked laugh and said: 'You've picked the wrong night for it, Pat. Everybody will be expecting you to.'

'True,' said McCoy, 'but that won't stop me.'

His friend put his hand on his shoulder and peered down into the dark stairwell with him.

'It's an advert,' said McCoy. Grogan cocked an eyebrow enquiringly. 'D'you not remember it? From the sixties. For Summer County margarine.'

'The Beethoven? Is it really? I didn't know that. Interesting.'

McCoy ignored Grogan and persisted with his theme: 'That's the difference between you and me, John. For you, it's Beethoven. For me, it's Summer County margarine. What good does it do me to know that it was used in an advert?'

'What good does it do me to know it's Beethoven?' countered Grogan, and brought their conversation to an end by tugging at McCoy's sleeve and pulling him up the remaining stairs

151

to MacRae's door. Grogan knocked purposively on the door, winked at McCoy and said in a penetrating voice: 'Thought Police. Open up.'

McCoy gave him a half-grin and started lah-lahing along to the Summer County Beethoven theme. As they heard a scuffling behind the door and a key rattling in the lock, Grogan joined in with the lah-lahing. MacRae's unshaven, worried face appeared in the half-open door. He always looked as if he had just woken up and wanted to go back to sleep as soon as possible, a demeanour made more emphatic by the most recent of his temporary jobs, as night guard in the Scottish Records Office, where he had leisure enough to ponder the Treaty of Arbroath in all its antiquated splendour.

Grogan pushed the door and MacRae to either side and marched into the flat followed by McCoy, both now lah-lahing to the music at full voice and in unison, until they stood on either side of the kitchen table at which MacRae had been working – there was his cup of tea, his tobacco, his ash-tray, his pen, his papers and his typewriter – swinging their arms to and fro like mad conductors and filling the room with their senseless shouting. MacRae followed them in and turned down the music. The oven door was open, this being MacRae's method of heating the kitchen. Above the cooker hung a shrivelled denim jacket, dogeared at the collar, frayed at the cuffs and patched here and there with scraps of different materials.

'Ah, the poet's coat of many colours,' observed Grogan, bowing at the knee and genuflecting to the jacket, 'Redcoat, bluecoat and turncoat.'

MacRae let the reference to his changing political affiliations – from S.N.P. to Labour and back again – pass. Grogan ripped the work-in-progress from the typewriter with a musical sweep of the arm, held the manuscript at arm's length and began to recite from it, then broke off to say in horror:

'Jesus Christ, this is prose!'

'You weren't working by any chance Ian, were you?' said McCoy.

'Well, aye, actually I was, but –'

'Of course he wasn't,' said Grogan. 'I mean look at this, it's all about a farm-hand being tried for buggering a cow in Perth in 1735, as far as I can see.'

152

He screwed up the typewritten sheet of paper from which he had been declaiming and threw it into MacRae's waste-paper basket, which was already laden with crumpled sheets of paper. 'Only a poet could work on the last day of the year.'

MacRae smiled briefly at the insult, then said: 'I suppose you two want tea.'

He stooped to retrieve the rejected manuscript, uncrumpled it enough to read over one or two of the lines he had written, then crumpled it up again and let it fall into the waste-paper basket and said, 'I'll save the reviewers the trouble.'

McCoy and Grogan laughed.

'Tea?' said MacRae.

'Something stronger,' said Grogan, reaching into his inside coat pocket.

MacRae saw the gold cap of the half-bottle as soon as it emerged from Grogan's pocket and, like a rodent emerging from hibernation, shook himself from the stuporous solitude of writing in an oven-heated kitchen with Beethoven on, and hurried to find three tumblers. 'You didn't think much of it, then?' He nodded to the crumpled paper in the waste-paper basket.

'I didn't think anything of it,' said Grogan.

'Neither did I,' added McCoy. 'I mean for christsake Ian, could you not have thought of a better subject to write about than that? Cattle-sodomy in Perth in 1735? It's hardly uplifting, is it, John?'

'I don't know,' said Grogan. 'It's got quite a lot going for it in terms of its marketability. A love interest. Scope for sexual fantasy. Historical content, that should get it into the tourist shops. A trial. An execution?'

MacRae smiled slyly and said, 'Aye. Two. They hanged the coo as well.'

Grogan clapped his hands together in delight.

'Wonderful. Do it from the cow's point of view, Ian, nobody's written anything from the point of view of an eighteenth-century cow in Perth. Where did you get the idea for it?'

'Call it *A Perthshire Puberty*,' put in McCoy.

'*The Perthshire Cowboy*,' suggested Grogan.

MacRae nodded gloomily, as if his own worst suspicions were confirmed and said, 'The thing is, it's a true story, it really happened, I read the account of the trial in the records office the other night.'

'Just because it's true,' said Grogan, 'is no reason to go and make it into fiction.'

'I was thinking it might make a play,' ventured MacRae.

'Oh yeah,' broke in McCoy, '*Daisy, daisy*, by Ian MacRae. A sensitive exploration of a young man's lust for livestock in Rural Scotland in the eighteenth century. Definitely prime time.'

'For all of the family,' urged Grogan, 'and their pets.'

MacRae laughed and yawned at the same time. He was used to their taunts.

'How's the job going anyway?' McCoy asked. He wouldn't have minded a number like that himself. MacRae made no secret of the fact that he was able to sleep on the job, make long-distance phone calls and sneak out to the pub, leaving the place and all the documents it housed unattended.

'Okay,' said MacRae. 'Except it's creepy in there at night. You keep thinkin you're hearing a ghost. And there's this wee room I'm not allowed to go into. I've not got a key for it.'

'How can you check it, then?'

'There's a wee window in the door, with mirrors on either side. You can see the whole room in the mirrors. I sometimes wonder what they keep in there.'

'State secrets,' said Grogan.

'Including the original recipe for stovies,' added McCoy.

MacRae smiled and said, 'I remember when I worked as an attendant at Lady Stairs House. One of the exhibits was an oatcake reputed to've been baked by Mrs Rabbie Burns. It's been taken down since.'

'There you are,' said Grogan, 'they've classified it as top secret material and put it in that wee room.'

MacRae laughed his low laugh that sounded more like sobbing, then he frowned at McCoy's sore eye and asked: 'What happened to you?'

As McCoy told the story of his meeting with Semple, MacRae nodded gloomily as if none of it surprised him in the least.

'So where'll you go now?' he asked, but Grogan held up his hand and declared:

'This is no time to plan for the future.' He poured three reasonable measures carelessly into the tumblers. 'A toast.'

'To what?' said McCoy.

'Ask the bard.'

McCoy and Grogan sat back in their chairs and looked at MacRae expectantly.

'A toast, let me think, now –'

Grogan and McCoy raised their glasses.

'To let me think now,' said Grogan.

They drank.

'And to let me go on thinking in the future,' added McCoy.

'And in the past,' added MacRae.

'Ah, the past. To our glorious past in all its solemn cattle-sodomy and splendour,' said Grogan, with satisfaction.

Another round of drinks was poured, and all three toasted the past, clinked their glasses and drank.

'May the past continue to haunt us as it always has done and always will do,' proposed McCoy.

'I can see the sense in that,' Grogan responded. 'But the real question is: Do the ghosts believe in us? If you were a ghost, would you?'

'They must, or they wouldn't hang about making noises in the Records Office,' said MacRae, reasonably.

'Talking about ghosts,' said Grogan, leaning over to MacRae, 'I've got something to tell you about our friend here, but it's for your ears only. Pat, would you excuse us for a minute?'

'Eh?'

'I'd like to have a word with Ian in private, if you don't mind.'

'What is this?' said McCoy. 'First you talk about me to two complete strangers in a pub –'

'And how d'you know we were talking about you?'

'It was obvious,' said McCoy. 'I heard my name.'

'Oh? And what makes you so sure you're the only person with your name? There could be another Patrick McCoy. We could have been talking about him, the other McCoy, the real one.'

Grogan refilled the glasses, raised his and said: 'To the other McCoy.'

'The other McCoy,' echoed MacRae. He smacked his lips after drinking as if he had begun to taste the secret. Then he held his glass out to Grogan to be refilled, saying: 'I've got to catch up wi you boys.'

'What other McCoy?' said McCoy, anxiously.

'Don't worry,' said Grogan, giving MacRae the extra refill he'd asked for, 'you'll find out when the moment is, eh . . .'

'Propitious?' suggested MacRae.

'Exactly the word,' said Grogan, sitting back in his chair and folding his arms and smiling and frowning at the same time. 'Propishous. Go for a pish, Pat.'

McCoy said: 'If it's something about me, some rumour that's going about . . .' – Grogan raised his eyebrows at MacRae and nodded frantically – 'I think I'm at least entitled to know what it's all about.' Grogan shook his head slowly.

'His lips are sealed,' observed MacRae.

'This is really childish,' said McCoy.

Grogan leaned towards him, looked into his eyes and, containing his mirth, said sincerely: 'It'll only take a minute.'

'Where am I supposed to go?'

'I made my suggestion.'

'What if I don't need a piss?'

'Have a secular genuflexion,' said Grogan, 'I don't care what you do, just leave us for a minute.'

'Okay, okay, but I think this is really childish of you both,' said McCoy, peevishly, as he rose from his chair and left the room.

He tried to hover outside the door, but Grogan followed him out and stood there until McCoy had gone into the toilet. As he was drying his hands he heard the loud laughter from the living-room, and as he went back in he knew that he had cut their conversation short.

He sat down at the table and pretended not to notice the conspiracy against him. Grogan and MacRae kept sneaking sly looks at each other and secretive grins.

MacRae opened his mouth to speak, but Grogan stopped him:

'Not a word now,' he warned.

'What the hell is it?' said McCoy.

'A little secret,' said Grogan.

'If you tell it to him, why can't you tell me it?' asked McCoy, peevishly.

'He knows I'm discreet,' said MacRae, smugly.

'That's right,' added Grogan.

McCoy scoffed and rolled his eyes.

'He knows that anything he tells me stops here,' said MacRae, tapping his chest with a finger, 'it reaches the ears of no one.'

'He'll probably stick it in one of his poems,' said McCoy.

'Then it's sure to reach the ears of no one,' said Grogan.

MacRae, caught off his guard, looked hurt by the insult. Grogan clapped him on the shoulder and said, 'Come on, Ian, I'm just trying to harden you up for the reviewers. How's the book doing, by the way?'

'Which one?' asked MacRae.

'Oh, it's like that, is it? You could do worse for a subject than this,' he nodded at McCoy. 'The *doppelganger*, I mean.'

'*Doppelganger*, what's that? That's German for something!' said McCoy, the accusation whining in his voice.

'Aye,' said MacRae, 'it's German for the other McCoy.'

Grogan went into an excruciating paroxysm of laughter, which developed into a fit of violent coughing, until McCoy had to thump him on the back while MacRae got a glass of water.

'Ah, Christ, I thought I wasn't going to see the New Year in there for a minute.'

'What's the plan anyway?' asked MacRae.

'Ah. Tonight.' said Grogan. 'Well, a few folk are meeting in the Café. Then there's a party at Tony McTaggart's place.'

'The Out-crowd again,' moaned MacRae.

'Can you think of anything better?'

MacRae shrugged, sighed heavily and shook his head.

'How about you, Pat? You heard of anything?'

'There's one in the New Town, not far from Yvonne's –'

'That's handy for you, eh?' put in MacRae. 'Whose is it?'

'Donald McDonald, the telly producer – the one who did *The Hogmanay Show*.'

'Of course, tonight's your big night, eh?' said MacRae. 'I could do worse than to come along to that. Does he need any script writers?'

Grogan held up his hand. 'I won't have you corrupted by the media as well as him, Ian. And what else, Pat?'

'Well, the one at Tony's. Apart from that, there's one away in Portobello, but to hell with that. *Puerta Belli!*'

'Too far away,' said Grogan. 'The important thing to decide is where we want to be at the bells.'

'New Year,' said MacRae, gloomily. 'I always tell myself I'm going to stay in, I'm going to ignore it, but I always get drawn into it. It's always an anti-climax, and it's always depressing, and I always get so pissed –'

'So why don't you go somewhere else, somewhere nobody knows you?' said Grogan, impatiently.

'I've tried that,' moaned MacRae, 'I remember one year, me and Julie, we went to Rome – I wanted to get away from the New Year here and that, but when I got there and when it came to the bells, this wee Scotsman came out in me and started shouting at everybody in the streets: 'C'mon, what'sa matter wi yez? It's New Year!' It was really embarrassing. Ended up wi three American sailors in a hotel room. By that time, Julie was up dancin on the table. Aye.'

Grogan rolled his eyes at McCoy and admonished: 'There'll be time enough for getting maudlin later on.'

'Scotland . . .' said MacRae, shaking his head and looking embarrassed but pleased by the memory.

'Scotland is a state of mind,' said McCoy.

'That's very true,' said MacRae.

'Who said that?' asked Grogan, suddenly alert.

'You did. At least I think it was you.'

'Did I? By Christ, I'll drink to that,' said Grogan and he poured the last of the half-bottle into their glasses.

'To Scotland as a concept,' said MacRae.

'No. A state of mind,' corrected Grogan.

'He's right, it's different,' said McCoy.

And they all toasted Scotland as a state of mind.

Grogan drained his glass and said decisively: 'Okay, let's get moving.'

'Where are we going?' said MacRae.

'The Café first.'

'It'll be jammed to the gills.'

'So what's new? We'll get in.'

'Then what – this producer's place, or what?'

'Where do we want to be at the bells?'

'We could go to the Tron.'

'Naw. Definitely not.'

'How? It's not far –'

'That's not the point –'

They went on discussing and disputing the best place to be at the bells as they left MacRae's flat and ran down the stairs.

Outside, the wind had a keen edge and there was a glaze of ice over the streets. The temperature had dropped, but McCoy didn't feel the cold, or the whisky inside him didn't. He'd had plenty to drink already, but he'd reached the point of no return.

They stopped at the off-licence to buy their bottles. It was as busy as hell and McCoy had to pay for his with the winnings from the fruit machine. Grogan and MacRae stood by the door waiting for him. He was aware of their smirkings and head-shakings as he counted out his coins.

On the way to the pub, he felt himself sink into a wallowing silence of self-loathing and even hung back a step or two behind his friends. He was going to be guttered by the time he met Yvonne, if he met her, and even on this night of all nights, that wouldn't go down too well under the circumstances. The thought of making the apologies to her filled him with dread: it was going to be like negotiating Salisbury Crags strung with land-mines on a foggy night. It might be easier to fall out with her completely and make an end of it – but who wanted to break up, on the last night of the year? Why did everything have to be so fucking difficult? Why was nothing in his life straightforward?

As they turned the corner into Hanover Street, he was stopped short by a sudden *déjà vu*. That bus shelter. That lamp-post. Here. He shouted to MacRae and Grogan, who turned round and came back to him reluctantly.

'What's up wi you?' moaned MacRae.

'It was here. Right here,' he said, pacing back and forth on the pavement.

'What was here?' asked Grogan, his curiosity beginning to quicken.

'It was definitely here. On the way home. After that party the other night. I stopped here. I remember it now. I met somebody . . . she . . . excuse me, have you got a cigarette?'

MacRae looked askance at Grogan, who pulled out his packet and gave McCoy a cigarette.

'That's it, just like that,' McCoy went on, 'she gave me a fag, I lit it –' Grogan struck a match and held it out to McCoy in his cupped hand. As he took the light, he remembered: 'Maggie Jordan! It was her I met, on the way home! I asked her for a cigarette, then I recognised her! I told her . . .'

'Who's she?' asked MacRae, losing interest.

'She's going out with Tony,' said Grogan to MacRae, with a meaningful nod of the head, then to McCoy: 'What did you tell her?'

'A lie . . . she believed me . . . but I can't remember what it was.'

McCoy was aware of Grogan whispering something to MacRae as he paced back and forth trying to rescue whatever it was from the murky depths of his memory.

'I've got to remember what I said,' said McCoy. 'It's important.'

'Aw let's get going,' said MacRae, 'it's freezing.'

'You'll remember later,' said Grogan, 'Anyway, she might be in the pub. You can ask her about it.'

McCoy reluctantly left the spot and followed his friends to the pub. Already people were yelling and singing in the streets, or else hurrying to pubs or houses to get as much serious drinking done as they could before the bells, but McCoy could not feel a part of it. Even when they approached the Café Royal and saw that it was packed solid – a situation that would normally make him all the more determined to get into the body of the bar and get a drink – McCoy felt as if he were being followed a few steps behind by a shadowy figure and he thought again about the other McCoy Grogan had joked about.

Grogan opened the door and they surveyed the crowded bar.

'For fucksake, John,' observed MacRae, 'Is it worth it?'

'Let's go somewhere else,' agreed McCoy.

'In we go!' cried Grogan, pushing both his friends down the steps and into the thick of it.

'THERE THEY ARE over in the corner,' said Grogan, 'Christ, they've got a table!'

'We'll never get served in here!' complained MacRae.

'Give me the money. I'll get them,' said McCoy.

'You'll be lucky to get them before closing,' persisted MacRae.

'Just watch me,' said McCoy.

So saying, McCoy struggled out of his coat and his jersey and handed them to MacRae. McCoy took the money, rolled up his sleeves and pushed his way between people to the nearest table, excusing himself briskly. He collected all the empty pint glasses on the table and stacked them into a long column, which he held between his two hands – one at the top and one at the bottom – and edged and shouted and bullied his way through the crowd towards the bar, every inch of him the harrassed barman. Even the black eye seemed to add authenticity to the performance.

The warmth and the lights and the noise annulled not only the cold night outside, but also the past and the future, and the press of bodies around him began to thaw him, and the hubbub and bustle of the bar made him feel good, part of this laughing, cursing, chattering, gesticulating, grinning, yelling, confiding, arguing, kissing, drinking, smoking, sweating swarm of humanity.

He wanted to watch and listen to every one of them so that he could do them all, so that he could learn to talk the way everyone talked, move the way everyone moved, look the way everyone looked, feel the way everyone felt, so that he could be one of them.

That must be why he did it. To be one of them. To be the

161

Other. He didn't want to be the real McCoy. He wanted to be the other McCoy.

'Excuse me, thank you –'

He pushed his way between them. Their smoke, their gaseous emanations and their voices filled the vaulted space of the bar, which was as resplendent as a church, with its carved and polished wood, its gleaming pictorial tiles, its imprinted mirrors and stained-glass windows.

So McCoy moved through the gathered multitude to the central oblong of polished wood in which the Spirit was enshrined, in the manifold upturned bottles, so precious a libation that it must be measured and meted out to the needy by His ministers on Earth – the bar staff. And thereby did The People stand aside to let him pass through, sensing the importance of his holy mission among them, to take back the empty glasses. He pushed between a young couple – 'Make way, please!' – and stood his offering on the counter.

'Oh ya beauty,' said the barman, quickly dismantling the column of glasses and upturning them two at a time in the trough of bubbling water below the bar, 'Just what we need.'

'Three pints. Three doubles,' said McCoy, between his hands, so that the people around him and behind him wouldn't hear. Even so he heard a deep voice behind him cursing him. But the barman gave him the nod as he pulled a pint and told him he'd get him in a minute.

'I'm here when you need me, Pat!'

McCoy turned round to see MacRae's anxious face behind him. He had a look of mad urgency in his dark eyes. Around him, all the anxious, angry, tired, scornful, disappointed, bewildered, mournful, resigned, bitter, outraged, hopeful faces wanted something, needed something: a drink, but that wasn't all it was.

He passed the drinks over to MacRae as they were poured, who passed them on to somebody else. Meanwhile additions to the order and fistfuls of pound notes were being passed the other way.

'Here he is!' cried Grogan, as MacRae and McCoy set the last of the round on the table, 'the real McCoy!'

Everyone sitting around the table raised their glasses and echoed Grogan's words. They were all there. The Out-crowd.

All except Yvonne and Maggie Jordan. They were all smiling up at him and cheering him. It felt good, but it felt like too much appreciation for a minor turn as a barman. Easy audiences were not to be trusted.

'But you've broken your resolution!' cried Grogan. 'He told me he'd made a resolution to give up impersonation and there he goes and mimics a barman!'

'In a good cause!' cried MacRae, tilting his glass to his lips.

'Anyway,' said Cathy Lyon, 'you can't break a resolution till after midnight.'

'Want a bet?' said Paul Haggerty.

'Break them before you make them,' said Tony McTaggart, 'eh Pat? That's the best way.'

Everybody kept looking at him strangely. They were all sitting except him. There wasn't a chair for him. It felt like being on stage. He didn't want to be on stage. Not like this. Not tonight.

People kept bumping into him and jostling him from behind. He caught sight of an empty chair at the next table, pushed his way over to it and shouted, 'Is anybody there?'

Someone waved a hand to tell him he could take the chair. He passed it over the heads of people to MacRae. He pushed his way back through the crowd and squeezed into the seat. He could still feel the crowd pushing against him from behind and sometimes someone would lean on his shoulder for support. Around the table, his friends were laughing at him again. Being funny when you didn't mean to be wasn't the way it was done.

'Is there anybody there?' said Helen Aitken, in the tone of an amateur clairvoyant, and the laughter erupted again.

'Watch it Pat,' said Hugh Mitchell, 'or you might make contact wi yourself!'

His slow, measured way of talking seemed to be the perfect delivery for the line, and their laughter took possession of them: Helen Aitken hooted and snorted; MacRae sobbed into his beer; Paul Haggerty squirmed around in his seat as the veins stood out on his temples; Cathy Lyon rocked back and forwards and made tight little fists of her hands, as if having to fight it; Hugh Mitchell shook it from his shoulders and brayed like a donkey in pain; Graham Pearson gargled and struggled for breath; Grogan doubled up and shuddered; Tony McTaggart did his am-dram repertoire, but like he couldn't help it for once.

163

Eventually, Grogan held up his hands.

'It's time we put the poor boy out of his misery. Tony, you better tell him.'

Tony McTaggart said: 'Pat, I'm really sorry about goin off like that when I saw you in the Dundas Arms.'

'What was all that about?'

'The thing is . . . I thought you were a –' but he couldn't get it out for laughing, and his laughter spread around the table. 'I thought you were a ghost!'

'A ghost?'

Tony went into another fit of laughter and everyone was infected by it. Everyone seemed dying to laugh anyway. Even some of the crowd of people standing near their table, who weren't in on the joke, joined in. It was the laughter people couldn't help, laughter that cleaned you out, laughter gone beyond its cause and come into its own, a thing in itself, laughter for the sake of laughter. It was what you prayed for. It was what made it all worthwhile. But did it? So many times in the past he'd wanted to join in with it, he'd felt himself weaken, felt the muscles at the sides of his face ache and his lips tighten as he struggled to keep the straight face you had to keep, because you were a comedian and you had to go on with the act, because it was your only defence, your only defence against the rush of the laughter that threatened to engulf you, to carry you away. Everyone needed it, needed to shout it loud from an open throat, bark it from a tossed head, wrench it in silence from an abdomen squirming to control its bladder, needed to giggle it throatily between teeth, between fingers, needed to howl it like a dog at the moon or gasp it like a breathless exasperation. It was why you got up there, why you stood in the spotlight and made a fool of yourself. All his life, he had needed it in others and feared it in himself. Now, he needed it himself and was beginning to fear it in the others. He wanted to join in. He wanted to feel its shuddering convulsions, feel it press his eyes shut to squeeze out two hot tears, feel it stretch his lips and show his teeth, needed to gasp for air and be doubled up with it. Needed to escape from himself. But he couldn't. The more he tried the more difficult it was. The fact that he didn't know what they were all laughing at didn't help.

'It's not funny,' said Cathy Lyon. 'We shouldnae laugh!'

'You tell him then!' cried Tony.

When the laughter prompted by this latest remark subsided, Cathy Lyon straightened her face and said:

'Well, Pat, I don't know how to tell you this, but there's been the most horrific rumour going round about you. We heard you were dead.'

'Dead?'

He looked around the faces, still twitching and contorting with laughter.

'You're kidding.'

'It's true,' said Grogan. 'We heard you'd committed suicide.'

'Eh?'

'Thrown yourself off the Dean Bridge!' shouted Graham Pearson, from the other side of the table.

'I heard it was an overdose. Somebody saw it in the paper yesterday,' said Cathy Lyon.

'I looked for it in the paper, but I couldn't see it,' said Helen Aitken.

A controversy arose over how he had done it, and how the rumour had come about in the first place.

'It must've been somebody else,' said Grogan, 'another Patrick McCoy. The other McCoy, Pat, eh?'

'Who told you I was dead?' said McCoy to the table in general, but he was feeling another *déjà vu*, as if he had dreamt all this long ago. His friends' voices came to him as if from far away, from some imagined future he'd lived through before.

'It was you told me,' said Cathy Lyon to Hugh Mitchell.

'She told me,' said Hugh, pointing the finger at Helen Aitken, who shook her head and held her hands up.

'It wisnae me!' she said, in the tone of one of her schoolkids, 'I heard from you, Tony. Pass the parcel.'

'It's like Chinese whispers.'

'Who told you, Tony?'

'Maggie did.'

'Maggie Jordan?' said McCoy.

'What's she got against you, Pat?' asked Graham Pearson.

'What about you, John?' said McCoy. 'Who told you I was dead?'

'Yvonne.'

'Yvonne thinks I'm dead?.'

'She did last night,' cried Grogan. 'She phoned me. I told you before, she said she'd never see you again and she cried a lot about it.'

'For christsake, John, a joke's a joke. You should've told me!'

'We didn't like to –' put in Tony.

'But Christ, John, is this what you were telling they women about in the Dundas Arms?'

Grogan nodded and beamed at him.

'And . . . Jan Pringle. Had she heard I was dead?'

Nobody seemed to know if Jan Pringle had heard or not, so McCoy described his meeting with her and how she'd acted. It was the mention of Maggie Jordan that clinched it.

'That's right,' said Helen Aitken. 'It was Maggie who told me.'

'Who told her?'

'I think she said it was your brother.'

'Eh? But I haven't seen my brother for years.'

'Who knows how rumours start,' put in Grogan.

'When am I supposed to have done it?'

'I heard it was yesterday morning,' said Cathy Lyon, with a shrug.

'I heard he did it on the way back from the party at your place, Hugh,' said Helen Aitken.

'Wasn't that bad a party,' said Hugh Mitchell. A ripple went around the table, then the hubbub of the crowd seemed to swell and engulf their conversation. McCoy had to shout to get his friends' attention.

'How did it start? I have to know!'

'Who told you about it, Ian?' Helen Aitken asked MacRae.

'Him,' said MacRae. 'I didn't hear about it until tonight.'

'The question you should be asking us,' said Grogan, 'is why you did it, not when.'

'Why did you think he did it?' asked Cathy Lyon.

'Well,' said Grogan, lighting a cigarette and taking a drink, as if signalling to everyone that this was going to take a while, 'I did ask myself that question this morning, before I went to bed. In fact, Pat, I was asking myself that question all night. The first motive I came up with was revenge.'

Hugh Mitchell moved around restlessly in his seat and said: 'How could suicide be revenge?'

'Ah, but usually it is, according to Camus anyway. Most people who do it really want to kill somebody else, but you'll be glad to hear, Pat, I didn't think you came into that category.'

'Why not?' said Hugh Mitchell. 'He could've been getting at Yvonne. I mean they've not been getting on, everybody knows that –'

'So what else is new – eh, Pat?' said Grogan.

McCoy shrugged. He was beginning to sweat. He didn't like this, the way his private life was being hauled out for everyone to have a look at.

'They have their ups and downs like everybody else,' put in Cathy Lyon in his defence, 'that doesn't mean he's gonnae top himself, does it?'

'Exactly,' resumed Grogan. 'It didn't merit the ultimate act of revenge. And if it wasn't revenge upon the Other, what was it? Revenge upon the self? That was my second theory. But that wasn't you either, Pat. Your Jekyll and your Hyde get on too well together.'

'Aw come on, John, just because you've been re-reading that book last night –'

'I turned to it in an attempt to understand you,' said Grogan. 'I was trying to make sense of your suicide.'

'He's not as bad as Jekyll-and-Hyde,' put in Graham Pearson, with a quick nod and a smile at McCoy.

'Thanks, Graham,' said McCoy, before Grogan continued:

'So. What else could have driven him to such a melodramatic act of self-effacement? It wasn't in character. Unless he was impersonating someone else at the time . . . But then, in that area you had no reason to be down in the dumps, what with your forthcoming appearance on the telly.'

'What's this, Pat?' said Graham Pearson, but before he could answer, MacRae told him to let Grogan finish.

'But then maybe that was it. Suicide as a form of stage-fright.'

'That's a bit far-fetched,' said Tony McTaggart. 'I mean, you'd already recorded it anyway, eh Pat?'

'Recorded what?' siad Graham Pearson.

'*The Hogmanay Show*,' said MacRae.

'I know he'd recorded it,' said Grogan, 'but it was still to be shown, that's the point. I mean maybe, since he'd recorded it, he knew in advance how bloody awful it was going to be and couldn't face the public humiliation of making a tit of himself on STV.'

'Plenty others do that every day,' said Paul Haggerty. Because he'd been sitting saying nothing, everyone looked at him when he spoke, as if expecting him to go on. Helen Aitken even nodded and smiled in encouragement, but Haggerty looked as if he regretted opening his mouth at all and bowed his head to let the attention turn away from him.

'And then I remembered you telling me, Pat, that you hadn't been paid for it yet,' continued Grogan, 'and I couldn't imagine you doing yourself in when you were waiting on a cheque.'

'Aw, that's not fair,' said Cathy Lyon.

'But then I wondered if money could be at the root of it somewhere.'

'I thought that as well,' admitted Hugh Mitchell.

'Me too,' said Helen Aitken.

'But I discounted that, on account of how, although you never have enough money, you don't care enough about it to jump off the Dean Bridge because of it. Which more or less left one with suicide as a metaphysical statement.'

'Oh aye, that,' put in Graham Pearson.

'But somehow I couldn't see you as the type to go in for the dark victory which annihilates earth and heaven.'

'So why did you think he did it, in the end?' asked Helen Aitken, clearly getting bored with Grogan's persistence.

Grogan held up a hand. 'I'm coming to it.'

'Don't rush,' said Hugh Mitchell, 'take your time.'

'Well,' said Grogan, 'then it ocurred to me that all my theories ignored the crucial factor: by all accounts he had been guttered when it happened.'

'Right,' said MacRae, 'he did it because he was blotto. That makes sense.'

Everyone seemed to nod and agree that this was a perfectly good explanation.

McCoy objected: 'I think I'd have to have some other reason than that. I mean, for Christ sake, folk don't kill themselves because they've had a few too many.'

'Ah,' said Grogan, 'maybe not, but in the case of Jekyll and Hyde –'

'Here we go again,' complained Graham Pearson.

'That's no a suicide case anyway,' said Hugh Mitchell.

'Isn't it?' said Grogan, standing up and pulling the book from his coat pocket and flicking through the pages. 'Listen to the last sentence: "I bring the life of that unhappy Henry Jekyll to an end." And that's Jekyll's own statement. And remember that Jekyll's transformation involved the taking of a drink.' He flicked through the pages until he found the one he wanted and declaimed the quote: ' "The mixture, which was at first of a reddish hue, began, in proportion as the crystals melted, to brighten in colour, to effervesce audibly, and to throw off small fumes of vapour. Suddenly, and at the same moment, the ebullition ceased, and the compound changed to a dark purple, which faded again more slowly to a watery green." '

'I'll have one of them,' said McCoy. 'Make it a double.'

Laughter.

'Who's round is it?'

'We'll split it.'

Grogan sat down and passed the book to Cathy Lyon. The conversation began to break up into several conversations, some of which still had to do with the rumour of his death, as money changed hands and MacRae and Haggerty organised the getting of the round.

It was strange to hear himself talked about as 'he', as if in a way he really had died, or part of him had. To be somebody. Somebody else. Somebody not himself.

His brother. This was the strangest thing. What could his brother have to do with it? For a moment McCoy entertained the idea that his elder brother could have deliberately started the rumour about him as some kind of weird mischief, but that wasn't in character and anyway he lived in Crawley and he didn't know any of his friends.

'Here, what happened to your eye?' Hugh Mitchell asked, on his way out to go the the toilet.

McCoy shook his head and said he didn't want to talk about it.

'Are you okay?' He leaned over and put a hand on his shoulder and the press of the crowd brought the two men closer.

'Well, apart from just hearing that I'm dead –'

Hugh Mitchell laughed and interrupted: 'Listen, Pat, I want to tell you something. You're a lucky bastard. See Yvonne? She really loves you.'

169

'Is that what she told you?'

'Naw. Well, aye. I mean, not in so many words, but. I mean, that's just how it looks to me.'

'You know something, Hugh, she's very fond of you as well. Listen, I'm really fucking sorry about the other night, by the way.'

'What for?'

'Aw, I was pissed.'

'So was everybody else. You were on good form, Pat.'

'Thanks, but I wasn't myself.'

'When are you ever, Pat?'

'I know, but I'd had a terrible row with Yvonne. Where is she, Hugh?'

'I haven't seen her since the party. Thought she'd be here the night though. Mibbe you should phone her, eh?'

He patted him on the shoulder and went on to the toilets.

'Christ. Has anybody –' McCoy raised his voice enough to make them all listen: 'Has nobody told Yvonne?'

'She knew,' said Grogan. 'She'd heard you were dead from somebody.'

'I told her,' said Helen Aitken.

'No! I mean, has anybody told her I'm not?'

There was a lull as everyone looked at each other. One or two hands covered mouths. There was the odd convulsion, the odd spasm of giggling, but everybody knew it wasn't very funny any more.

Grogan said: 'You definitely better tell her, Pat.'

'Where is she?' said McCoy.

Everybody looked at each other, but nobody knew.

'Think of it, Pat,' said Grogan. 'The last time you saw her you had a blazing row, right? Then she hears you're dead. What would she do?'

'She's probably sitting in her flat crying her eyes out,' said Helen Aitken.

'So,' went on Grogan, 'think of it, Pat. What a first foot that would be – back from the dead!'

But Cathy Lyon and Helen Aitken wouldn't hear of the idea. They were shaking their heads and looking deadly serious.

'Go and phone her, Pat. D'you want me to do it?' said Helen Aitken.

McCoy stood up and pushed his way towards the phone in the corner of the bar. He dialled the number.

Yvonne, it's me. I'm alive. That was all he had to say. Anything else would be frills. He wanted there to be no frills, no jokes, no guessing games, no room for misunderstanding. I'm alive. Anyway, he'd have trouble making that much heard above the hubbub behind him. He held the phone tightly to his ear. He had to hear her reaction. It would be the test. The real test. He dreaded it. But she was engaged. So at least she must be there. He tried again. Still engaged. He fought his way downstairs to the toilets, nodding to Hugh Mitchell on his way back up.

Waiting in line to pee, he was aware of all the repartee going on around him, but he couldn't feel a part of it, couldn't join in. Yvonne thought he was dead. What did that mean? It meant that he was, that a part of him was. And wasn't that what death was, or a part of it? People hearing that you were.

He battled his way upstairs and phoned her again. Still engaged.

When he got back to the table, there was a little queue of whiskies at his place, waiting for him.

'Did you get her, Pat?'

'She's engaged.'

'She must've left it off the hook,' said Helen Aitken.

'Oh no,' said Cathy Lyon, covering her mouth with her hand and, incidentally, letting the other hand fall on Haggerty's arm. Graham Pearson glanced quickly at the offending gesture and looked sick. So the night's alignments were beginning to take shape already. But Yvonne wasn't there, had left the phone off the hook, might be pregnant and thought he was dead.

It's all so horribly complicated, Mr McCoy. Tell him he's not funny any more . . . His landlord's words echoed and distorted in his drunken brain as the resentment swelled inside him.

'This is all your fault, Grogan. You should've told me earlier.'

The anger in his voice made it go high and everyone around the table fell silent. The clamour of voices around them seemed to swell. Grogan looked taken aback.

'I'm sorry, Pat! It was only a joke! Don't worry about it! We can go to her place after the pub. She'll be delighted to see you!'

'What about the party?' said Helen Aitken. 'Will she not be coming?'

171

'Would you, if your boyfriend had died?' said MacRae.

'I haven't got a boyfriend,' said Helen Aitken, tilting her head in the parody of a coquette and batting her eyelids.

'That sounds like a declaration of intent,' said MacRae.

'It is,' said Helen Aitken, giving MacRae a steady look that made him flinch visibly and change the subject:

'Where are we going, anyway?'

'My place,' said Tony.

'What about this producer's party?' MacRae asked.

'Whose?'

'How about the Tron?'

'Christ, no!'

Already there were signs of dissension. Some wanted to go directly to Tony's, others wanted to take in the Tron first, and MacRae was doing his best to persuade Grogan and McCoy to go to the producer's place, then on to Tony's. Haggerty was all for the Tron, Graham Pearson was for going straight to Tony's.

'Aye, let's go to the Tron,' said Cathy Lyon. So she was bombing Pearson out and going for Haggerty. Helen Aitken was waiting to find out what the consensus was, impatiently, because there was none.

'This is the fuckin trouble wi this country,' Haggerty said abruptly, 'we cannae agree about anythin.'

'What about the last election?' said Hugh Mitchell. 'We were unanimous enough then.'

'Aye, to give the government the v-sign, that's all,' Haggerty replied, 'and where's that got us?' He looked at his watch. 'I think I'm gonnae get the last train to Glasgow.'

'Don't do that, Paul,' said MacRae, 'you'll end up celebrating it in Linlithgow. Happened to me once.'

'Defeatist talk,' put in Grogan. 'We're so used to being defeated, we've forgotten how it feels to win.'

'They wouldn't've tried the Poll Tax in Northern Ireland, that's for sure,' said Cathy Lyon.

Haggerty agreed with her passionately.

'Don't get the train, Paul, eh?'

They began their courtship there and then with a complicated discussion of the Poll Tax issue and all its ramifications. Occasionally Graham Pearson chimed in to dispute something

172

Haggerty said, but it was clear that he wasn't really being listened to.

'I quite fancy the Tron,' said Grogan. Though he was talking to the table in general, he was looking at McCoy, who was sulking conspicuously.

'Not me,' said McCoy. 'You know what it's going to be like, so why bother?'

'I don't. Every year's different. If you think like that, Pat, you'd be as well dead.'

'What about this producer's party?' said MacRae.

The disputes went on. Everyone was beginning to feel tense and irritable. McCoy clammed up and worked his way through the whiskies. It was an effort to keep listening to people trying to make themselves heard above the general clamour of the bar.

'Tony's!' cried Graham Pearson.

'Naw, the Tron!' cried Haggerty.

'There's plenty time to decide yet,' said Cathy Lyon. But there wasn't. Not for her. Not for anyone. Not tonight, not any night. They were all getting older.

McCoy looked around the bar. Already the barmen were beginning to look at their watches.

IT WAS WHAT was happening at the time, but it wasn't like now. It was what was going on around him, but it had a wobbly quality, as if the solid floor they stood on, and the foundations below, were slowly sliding into a bog of seismic mud and the fossilised fish-suppers of centuries. The party was not what he'd expected. Not that he'd expected a foostie oatcake affair with the trays of sherries and the black bun and the plates of sandwiches on the sideboard quite, but somehow he'd imagined that Donald McDonald's party would be a fairly sedate affair.

It was not. Even on the way along the street there had been the feeling that they were part of an unruly procession of revellers, and as they'd neared the house they'd realised that the procession was going to the party. The place was packed with all kinds of people, as if three very different pubs had heard about the party and had decided to come along. Maybe that was what had happened. To add to the confusion, there were lit candles on every available surface, which were always being knocked over and dripping hot wax everywhere. Apart from the kitchen, the producer's spacious, tattered New Town flat was in virtual darkness.

McCoy, MacRae, Paul Haggerty, Grogan, Helen Aitken and Cathy Lyon pushed their way into the kitchen, in the hope that the hub of the party would be in there. It wasn't. In the corner, sitting on a pile of old newspapers, a fiddler was playing a reel and somebody else was thumping out a rhythm with a wooden spoon and a biscuit tin. Apart from that everyone seemed to be looking for something or someone, so that there was the atmosphere of a busy railway station. Donald McDonald knew lots of people, apparently, but most of them didn't know each other and didn't

174

much want to.

They occupied a corner, got hold of some paper cups and a bottle of wine and got started.

'I don't know anybody here,' complained Cathy Lyon.

'Neither do I,' said McCoy.

'Neither does anybody else,' put in Grogan.

'This is hellish,' said MacRae. 'Who's idea was it to come here?'

'Yours,' said McCoy.

'What are we doing here?' asked Cathy Lyon.

'Let's get the hell out,' said Paul Haggerty. 'Lets go to the Tron.'

'No, let's go to Tony's' said Cathy Lyon, more to Haggerty than anyone else.

'Aye, it might be less crowded at the Tron right enough,' said MacRae.

'Right,' said Haggerty, 'are we all agreed, then? We're going to the Tron.'

'What about Yvonne?' said Cathy Lyon. 'You were going to phone her, Pat.'

'I'll go and get her. I can't face the Tron,' said McCoy.

'We'll see you back at Tony's.'

They went on arguing about it until the milling of the crowd split them up. Grogan and McCoy were left to finish off the bottle. Grogan put his arm round McCoy and said:

'I was quite cut up when I heard you were no longer with us. No, honest. That's why I went to the Dundas – to drown my sorrows. Ach, you're not still annoyed at me, are you? Okay, I should've told you about the rumour. I wanted to save it. I couldn't resist it. I wanted it to be a surprise.'

'You weren't the only one,' said McCoy, gloomily. 'Tony could have told me when he saw me. So could Jan Pringle.'

'I wanted to deliver you from the grave. A pity Yvonne wasn't in the Café. Have you tried phoning her again?'

'Not yet. Christ. I suppose I better get along there and sort it out. You want to come, John?'

'Me? Why should I come?'

'You said you'd go and see her, didn't you?'

'That was last night, Pat – when we thought you'd croaked. I thought someone should go and, you know –'

175

'Comfort her? Hold her hand? Help her through her grief?'

Grogan took a step back, looked at McCoy askance, clapped a hand on his shoulder and laughed.

'You've a suspicious mind, Patrick McCoy!'

But it pleased him to have been thought of as an object of suspicion.

'So would you if you spent your day trying to flog spy-holes while the rumours were flying round about you. Tell me honestly, John – did you start it?'

'For Christ sake, Pat, get a grip of yourself. No. And I was going to see Yvonne because she asked me to. She wanted to see me because I was your friend. She thought you were dead, Pat.'

'How did she take it?'

Grogan sighed and leaned so close to McCoy that their faces almost touched.

'How d'you think?'

'Tell me.'

'She was cut up about it.'

'Is that all?'

'Really cut up. Devastated. What d'you want me to say?'

'What did she look like, what was her face like?'

'Christ, Pat, we were on the phone!'

'I forgot. Did she sound really devastated?'

'She thought you were dead, Pat.'

'She probably still does.'

'All the better! Go and get her. Sort it out.'

'Come with me, John.'

'You don't want me there, Pat, it's between you and her. Don't look so down in the mouth. She'll be over the moon, I'm telling you! Back from the dead, I'm telling you, when she opens the door – imagine her face!'

'You should've told me, John.'

'I did! I just held it over till we met the others. C'mon, Pat, stop thinking about it, eh? It's New Year. It was just a joke. If you can't take a joke, who can?'

Grogan brought his hand from McCoy's shoulder and held it out. McCoy relented and shook it. Grogan did not let go. He kept on shaking McCoy's hand and staring into his eyes with a drunken meaningfulness, until MacRae shoved through the crowd to them.

'We've decided. We're off to the Tron. Are you coming, or what?'

Grogan drank the last of his wine, grimaced and said, 'Time to go!'

'I'll see you later.'

They tried to persuade him to go with them and made him promise to come to Tony's later, bringing Yvonne with him. When Grogan drew away from him he looked at him portentously, as if he was making a grave error by staying behind.

'Don't get morbid, now,' said Grogan, with a twisted smile.

When they'd gone, he opened a can of beer and drank it down quickly. He opened another and began to edge his way from one room to another. People had started to sort themselves out and quite a few had apparently taken one look and left. But there was nobody he recognised. He opened another can and looked at people as he moved from room to room. Everyone seemed to be pretending to be something they weren't. His thirst was unslakeable. He was drunk, he must be drunk, but he wasn't drunk enough to face Yvonne at her door. He didn't relish the moment that Grogan was so enthusiastic about: Yvonne's face when she opened the door. The shock of seeing him alive. He found his way to the phone in the hall. This time it rang. It rang and went on ringing. She wasn't there or she wasn't answering. As he put the phone down a hand gripped his arm.

'My dear boy . . . you're alive!' said Donald McDonald, and he looked aghast, as if it troubled him deeply. He made a slow-motion pantomime of his agitation, grasping a clump of the lank grey hair that spilled over his horn-rimmed glasses and rounding his eyes in a parody of horror. 'But aren't you . . . I mean to say, you're the one who . . . Well I'm bleeeeped.'

'Eh?'

Donald McDonald explained his eccentric habit of censoring his own profanities with a bleeping noise like those used on t.v.

'Oh,' said McCoy, 'I see. But don't tell me you heard I was dead as well?'

'You're the one who's been . . . edited out.'

'I know, there's been a rumour going round. I don't know how it started – you know what Edinburgh's like. Probably some other McCoy.'

'Other McCoy?'

'The one who died, I mean'.

'Died? But you're not dead.'

'A case of mistaken identity. Some other McCoy must have died.'

'Ah ha.'

The way the man's bewildered stare struggled to hold him in focus, then slid off him to the floor, let McCoy know just how pissed the producer was. But it was as if he was playing at being pissed as well. He had so many mannerisms that he was never at rest for very long, but constantly pointing a finger or running a hand over his grey goatee beard or raising his eyebrows or nodding his head. It was all exaggerated by the drink as he led McCoy through the crowded party to a room that wasn't so busy.

'The study,' said Donald McDonald.

A t.v. was on in the corner, but the sound was drowned out by music from another room and the garbled noise of many conversations going on at once. The producer sat down heavily in a tattered leather armchair. He looked vaguely at all the people sitting and standing around, as if wondering who the hell they were. He picked up a glass of whisky from a small table by his chair and motioned loosely to McCoy. 'Grab a pew, old son.'

McCoy found a stool and pulled it up beside the producer's armchair. As he talked, the whisky twisted his face into a caricature of itself, stretching his grins wider and deepening his much deliberated frowns.

'Patrick. You are a young man of some . . .' Here he paused for a long time and seemed to gaze into the far distance, as if the next word had only just appeared on the horizon and wasn't near enough to be deciphered. 'Ah . . . value. You have the talent. You have the voice. You have the face. You have the timing. And more important, you've got the . . .' – he looked into the distance again, but this time swung his gaze to take in the bottle of whisky McCoy was tugging out of his pocket and opening – '. . . the *bottle*. Don't mind if I do.' He held out his glass and McCoy refilled it. Having no glass himself, McCoy swigged it from the bottle. The producer went on: 'I mean, the bottle to get up there and give the bleepers what they don't bleeping want, right?'

'Well, I suppose so –'

Donald McDonald closed his eyes, rolled his head backwards and held up a hand.

'No supposing about it. You and me, we're educators. Shape the sensibility of the nation – d'you see what I'm saying? Now. *The Hogmanay Show*. Difficult to be political on *The Hogmanay Show*. Your spot was wonderful, although we did have to cut out that reference to the Poll Tax. Not what people want to hear about at Hogmanay, laddie. And I mean even if you're not political, that's a political choice too nowadays, wouldn't you agree? But that wasn't what was wrong with your spot. I personally enjoyed that bit about the Poll Tax, but –'

'But you cut it?'

'No, I didn't cut anything. Nothing. Not me, personally. Your spot was wonderful, we'd decided to use most of it, but . . . You see, *The Hogmanay Show* . . . Awful title. D'you want to know the truth? I wanted to re-title it. *The Bells*. What d'you think?'

'Well . . . it's nice and simple.'

'Simple. Direct. To the point, that's what I'm getting at, you see. You understand what I'm trying to tell you? But would they let me? Would they bleep. But it's changing. I'm changing it. One day. There's not a dearth of talent. It's not that. Well, even if there is a dearth of talent, that's not the trouble. Take you. Your spot was terrific. Really, really terrific, Patrick. Point is, I heard you were dead, old son. All right, nothing wrong with that. Some of my best friends are dead. Matter of fact . . . they're all, how can I put it? Dead. You're a young man, Patrick, at least you're still alive. You're not dead, I can see that perfectly clearly. It's a bleeping shame really. Mind if I help myself?' He took the bottle and sloshed another treble into his glass. 'Of course, everyone knows it isn't live. I know that. I make no secret of the fact. How can I? You know as well as I do. But the point is . . . it really is very unfortunate, my dear, dear boy . . . but you see, the fact of the matter is . . . we have to maintain, we have to . . . preserve the time-honoured illusion, if you get my point. Oh don't get me wrong old son, I personally don't give a monkey's bleep for our time-honoured illusion. But it's there. Up there. You see, when everyone joins hands and pretends . . . that it really is twelve o'clock midnight. The bells. And then they sing *Auld Lang Syne*, as you know . . . I mean you were there, you did it . . . Oh bleeping hell. I forgot you were in the bleeping auld lang syne

179

scene. Bleep me. Too late, too late – anyway, what could I do? I couldn't cut the bleeping finale, could I?'

'Cut the finale?'

'When I heard you'd popped off. I had to get on the phone to Glasgow. Emergency edit, my dear boy. Out out, damned spot.'

'Emergency edit? You mean . . . my spot . . .'

The producer nodded gravely and drew his finger over his throat. 'Oh, and an announcement. I'm afraid so. Due to the tragic untimely blah blah, so on and so forth . . . Patrick McCoy . . . will regrettably not be taking part as advertised . . . Well, you'll see it for yourself. It'll be on soon.'

'I've been edited out.'

'That's what I've been trying to tell you.'

'Shit.'

'I know how you must feel, no matter, a man of your calibre. There will be other spots.'

'Bastard,' said McCoy.

The producer looked as if he had been slapped across the face by a mosquito.

'No need to be unpleasant,' he said.

'I don't mean you. I mean whoever started this bloody rumour about me. Jesus. Everyone watching will think . . . Can't you put on another announcement?'

The producer closed his eyes and shook his head slowly.

'Too late now. Tomorrow maybe.' Suddenly he perked up at the thought of a little publicity. 'We could get something in the paper, in next week's *Radio Times* –'

'Who told you?'

'Mmm? Oh! Your young lady called to tell me.'

'Yvonne?'

'That's her. Sounded terribly upset about it all. I trust you've put her right?'

'She phoned you today?'

'Yes. She was very definite about it, I must say. I do hope she's all right –'

McCoy stood up abruptly and said that he had to go. He hurried out into the hall and, disorientated, couldn't find the door out. He looked into another crowded room. People were talking and laughing and clutching each other and kissing in there. In the centre of all the activity there was a man who was sitting perfectly still, talking to no one and staring straight at him.

'Semple!'

A few of the people in the room turned to look at him. Semple raised his glass slowly and smiled at him affably.

McCoy glared with barefaced hatred at his landlord, who sat there smiling affably, now holding out his glass to be refilled by the Wholesaler.

When the Wholesaler looked over his shoulder at him, McCoy ran. Out the door and down the steps into the street. Holding his bottle in his pocket, he kept running until he reached her close. He leaned against the inside of the door to regain his breath before going up.

Yvonne. It's me. I'm alive. No. He didn't have to say anything. He just had to see her, to be seen by her.

He climbed the stairs slowly and rang her doorbell.

No answer. He leaned against the door and battered on it with the side of his hand. Nothing. She was out. Then, he heard a noise somewhere inside. Something had stirred. He knelt down and peered through the letterbox.

He saw Jinx crouched in the doorway to her bedroom, head down, glaring up at him suspiciously.

'Jinx! What the hell are you doing in there?'

The cat miaowed smugly, licked her lips, yawned and rearranged her position.

'Yvonne! Are you in there?'

There were lights on but she wasn't there. She'd left in a hurry. On an impulse. Did she still think he was dead, or had one of the others got through to her to tell her he wasn't?

Where would she go?

Out in the street, he asked a man hurrying past him what time it was. Twenty minutes to go. He could get there if he hurried.

HE COULD SENSE it before he reached Princes Street, the way people were hurrying towards it, as if they couldn't help themselves. He felt it too, drawing him up the Mound as fast as he could walk without breaking into a run. And he heard the human din of its thousand voices above the High Street, a communal roar that became suddenly much louder as he turned the corner at the top of the Mound. He had forgotten what it was like. The High Street was choc-a-bloc from St Giles to the Tron. Even from here he could see that the big hand was closing in on the little one. Only a few minutes to go. He pushed between people, looking for Yvonne or Grogan or MacRae. Somebody. He moved through the turbulent crowd this way and that, but couldn't see anyone.

A shrill laugh sounded on his right and he moved in its direction. Then there was a deep belch of laughter behind him, so he turned round and tried to see where it came from. Then he could hear it everywhere, on all sides, sometimes an inch from his ear and other times some way off, scattered laughter that was mixed up with shouting and screaming and groaning and crying. It wouldn't go away. It wouldn't leave him alone.

The real McCoy wanted to find her, but the other McCoy wanted to be found. The real one wanted to take part in the festivities, the other one had seen it all before. He pushed his way through the crowd to the Christmas tree outside St Giles and looked up at it. Then he remembered Willie Turnbull's story of the year he'd climbed it. He looked down at the dead man's shoes on his feet and laughed. It was a way out. It seemed like a good idea. If Willie Turnbull could do it, so could he.

He took a long swig from his bottle, then pushed over one of the crash-barriers, stuck the bottle back in his pocket and stepped up

182

to the tree. He pulled himself up into the branches. He climbed quickly, until he was as high as he could go, then wedged himself between two branches near the top. He got his breath and felt the cold night air nip his eyelids and his lips. The wind lifted the branches under his feet and rolled them around and made the lights dance around him. He was dimly aware of people pointing up at him. Someone was waving, but no one he knew, just a face in a sea of faces, one of the audience. He managed to take out his bottle and unscrew the cap. Now more people were turning to point up at him and shout to him and some were clapping and cheering.

He looked down at the upturned faces of the crowd. The crowd of pissed strangers. It was out of control. It was an audience looking for the show. It was a Shakespearean audience. Discerning. It discerned between what it liked and what it hated, what it cheered and what it booed. It was good enough for McCoy.

The tree sways a little in the wind, and he feels himself swaying with it as he holds his arm out, at the end of which is a hand, in which is held a bottle of whisky, and he holds it out there so that it catches the Christmas tree lights and the amber turns to molten gold, and as he brings the bottle to his lips he loses sight of it, so that his lips have to guess where the mouth of the bottle is, then he upturns it with a quick flick of the wrist and drinks and lets the whisky sing O Danny Boy, the pipes, the pipes are calling, from glen to glen . . . and the discordant chorus of shouts and hoots, shrieks and whistles, cheers and boos rises up to meet him, and for a moment he knows how Hamlet feels when the schoolkids stamp their feet and he tells them to shut up, and he shouts and goes on shouting out into the darkness with the panted steam of his breath:

'Spy-holes! Spy-holes! Come and get your spy-holes! Only three quid! The Complete Service, parts included! You see out – they don't see in! I could've been anyone! I'm not dead yet! I'm still alive! You owe everybody in this room an apology! Right now! I'm not free yet! I'm still my father's son! Ye think Ah'm a bastardin orphan, eh? So was Jesus Christ of fuckin Nazareth! Yvonne, Yvonne, I didn't mean it! Edit me out! Go ahead! The real McCoy! What about me! What about the other McCoy!'

'Who's he?' somebody yelled from the crowd.

'He's *me*.'

The words were lost in the chorus of hoots and whistles and jeers, then the night erupted into a chaos of shouting and cheering and singing. The bells were sounding, though their chimes were swallowed by the uproar. McCoy, swaying among the dancing lights, heard a snatch of the *Auld Lang Syne* and felt suddenly very alone and cold and scratched and sore and drunk and tired and hungry and sorry for himself.

They were all cheering and clapping and kissing and shaking hands and passing the bottle but the whole scene began to blur as the tears streamed from his eyes.

He took another pull at his bottle, then put the cap on. As he tried to put it back in his pocket, the world lurched and the bottle jumped from his hand, crashed through the branches and the lights and exploded on the cobbles below. A piercing scream punctured the general uproar, then someone was shouting to him to come down. But it was harder to climb down than up and his arms and legs began to shake with the effort. He thought he heard his name called, but he dared not look.

When he was near enough, he dropped to the ground. Someone tugged and his sleeve and he turned round.

'Happy New Year, Yvonne.'

The world reeled around them as they kissed and he felt her shoulders shudder in his arms and the hot brine of her tears stinging his bruised eye. She pulled back from him to look at him and laugh and shake her head and say his name and tell him he was alive, and he believed her, as if he really had died and come back from the dead.

She kept telling him that she'd thought he was dead, that everyone thought he was, and he kept telling her that he knew, that it was a malicious rumour and that he was sorry. He went on saying he was sorry over and over again until it was true.

'It's New Year,' she told him. 'You're not allowed to be sorry.'

THE PARTY WAS in full swing when they arrived, but McCoy was in no condition to take the taunts and the jibes thrown his way as they made their way into the kitchen.

'It was announced on telly, Pat,' said Tony McTaggart. 'You're dead.'

'I know, I know, they edited me out. Due to the untimely death, blah blah blah . . . Patrick McCoy will not be taking part as advertised.'

'You were in the finale, singing *Auld Lang Syne* with the rest of them though,' said Tony McTaggart. 'I've got it on video, if you want to see yourself! By the way, have you met Maggie? I think you want to anyway, eh?'

He was aware of Grogan and MacRae, over at the drinks table, telling people to shush. Then he thought he heard somebody holding in their laughter. The conspiracy against him was still afoot, it seemed.

'Hello, John,' said Maggie Jordan, pushing in beside Tony. Grogan and MacRae turned away to contain their laughter.

'My name's Pat. Listen, tell me what all this is about, eh? Somebody said – it was you, Tony! – that you told them I was dead.'

Maggie Jordan smiled at him simply and answered, 'I did.'

'Who told you?'

'Your brother.'

'My brother? But he's in Crawley!'

'The other one,' said Maggie Jordan.

'But I don't have another brother!'

'Are you sure about that?' put in Tony McTaggart. 'Maggie met him, eh Maggie?'

185

'The other McCoy!' Grogan and MacRae cried in unison from the drinks table.

'It was you I met, wasn't it? On the way home from Hugh's party. I asked you for a cigarette . . .'

Maggie Jordan nodded and laughed.

'You told me, Pat.'

'Eh?'

'I recognised you from that time in the pub, but you denied it – you said you'd never met me before. Said your name was John McCoy and that you were often mistaken for your brother Pat, who'd only just died! A terrible case, you said. Suicide!'

'I did not!'

'And she believed him!' Grogan cried from the drinks table.

The room erupted in laughter and he felt it flood into him until he couldn't help letting go and joining in, letting the laughter that was his and no one else's shake him senseless and clean him out. Then it took over and he couldn't control it, until no one else was with him, he was laughing alone, and still he couldn't stop. His ribs ached. His lungs gasped for air. He shuddered. He sweated. When he saw that Yvonne wasn't laughing at all but looking distinctly pissed off with him, his laughter became all the more painful and uncontrollable, as if her anger was the final comic touch in the whole absurd situation. Even when she walked out of the room, the laughter had rendered him helpless to do anything about it. Eventually, Grogan sat him down and handed him a whisky.

'And you suspected me of starting malicious rumours about you – when it was you yourself, Pat McCoy.'

McCoy wiped his streaming eyes on his sleeve and began to recover. He kept half-hearing snatches of what Grogan was saying, like 'The question is – who died? The real McCoy, or the other one?' and 'It wasn't suicide. It was assassination. You assassinated the part of yourself that was willing to appear on *The Hogmanay Show*, and a good thing too . . .'

'Maybe it was my last joke,' said McCoy and he didn't wait for Grogan's answer, but went to find Yvonne.

She was dancing with Hugh Mitchell and pretended not to see him coming into the room. He waited for her, even though she stayed up for another number. He caught her by the arm as she made to walk out of the room.

186

'What's wrong, Yvonne?'

'What's wrong? You're a compulsive liar, that's what's wrong. You start a rumour that you're dead, you get everybody upset – I've been through hell since I heard – then you laugh when you find out and then you don't think you've done anything wrong! You laugh about it!'

'I couldn't remember saying it, Yvonne, it was on the way back from Hugh's party, I was drunk.'

'That's supposed to be an excuse for everything.'

'Ach, I must've just said it for fun. I didn't think she'd go telling everybody –'

'Well she did.'

'How was I to know? Look Yvonne, I was cut out of *The Hogmanay Show* because of it – and that was your fault! I've learned my lesson, or do you have another punishment excercise in mind?'

It was starting to get nasty and people were already edging away from them. Hugh Mitchell pretended to be looking through the records as he waited to see the outcome.

'What about your mother? Have you thought about that?'

'You didn't phone her and tell her as well, did you?'

'I couldn't find out her number, or I would've!'

'Anyway, I phoned her earlier. She hadn't heard I was dead.'

'What about the announcement?'

'Oh Christ, I hadn't thought of that.'

He took the phone on its wire from the hall into the room being used for coats, shut the door and dialled the number and waited. He heard his mother's anxious voice reciting her phone number.

'Mum, it's me.'

'Patrick! What is it, son?'

'I'm alive, Mum.'

'What time is it? Oh Patrick, what are you phoning for at this time? You're worse than your dad. I was in my bed asleep!'

'I'm sorry Mum – did you not hear the announcement on the t.v.?'

'What announcement?'

'On *The Hogmanay Show*.'

'Aw son, I fell asleep in my chair before it came on – I missed your thing. But I woke up just at the bells and I saw you singing the *Auld Lang Syne*. You were awful good, son.'

187

'Is that right? I'm sorry for waking you up, Mum, it's just that there was this announcement about me before the show came on, saying I'd died. People thought I was dead –'

'Aw, away ye go, they did not.'

'They did Mum, there was a rumour, and the t.v. people heard about it, so they cut out my act. I just wanted to phone you in case you heard the announcement, that's all, to tell you that I'm alive –'

'I know you're alive, son.'

'I know you do, Mum.'

He could tell the talk of death was beginning to distress her by the way she was sniffing into the phone.

'Thanks for the ten quid, by the way.'

'Get yourself a good pair of shoes, son.'

'I already did, Mum.'

'What like are they?'

'They're dark tan imitation brogues, Mum.'

'Imitation? Did you not have enough for the real ones?'

'I like the imitation ones better, Mum.'

'Well I hope they've got good soles on them, son.'

'The soles are great, Mum.'

'That's good.'

'What did I look like, Mum, singing *Auld Lang Syne*?'

'You looked just like yourself, son.'

'Did I really?'

He couldn't think of anything else to say, so he wished her a happy New Year again and promised to go to see her soon.

'Happy New Year, son.'

He still wasn't sure if she'd understood about the rumour and the announcement. He still wasn't sure if he had. He sat among the coats, going over it all gloomily until Yvonne came looking for him.

'Did you get her?' He nodded. 'Did she hear it?'

He shook his head but didn't make it look like he was telling her she'd been wrong to worry. She sat down beside him and lit a cigarette. There was a strained silence, as McCoy tried to find a way to bring the subject up.

'Come on then Yvonne, tell me.'

'Tell you what?'

'Are you or aren't you?'

'I could've been.'

'So you're not?'

'No.'

'When did you find out?'

'Tonight. When I was having a bath. My period came.'

He sighed with relief, then regretted it.

'You didn't really think you were, did you?'

'Maybe not, but you know what happened as well as me.'

'I was there at the time, Yvonne.'

'And I was late. So. I could've been. I didn't *know*.'

'What would you have done?'

'I'd decided to have an abortion.'

'That makes sense.'

'Then I heard you were dead. Then I wondered if maybe I should have it. I mean, I might not have another chance.'

'You've got plenty time yet –'

'No I don't.'

He put his arm round her. Though she moved a little bit closer she gave him a look to let him know she wasn't happy.

'So you really did think I was a goner.'

'I even went round to the shed today and got Jinx.'

'I know! I saw her! Through the letterbox! Jesus! That cat is an opportunist. She's making my decisions for me!'

'What decisions?'

'Decisions about my life, you know.'

'Oh, them.'

'I mean, why can't I choose something until I feel that I can't do anything else, until there's no choice?'

'That's just the way it is.'

He pulled her closer to kiss her, but she pulled back to ask:

'Are you not even a bit sorry?'

'It's New Year. I'm not allowed to be.'

LATER, WHEN THE party had worn down to the hard core of the dancers and the drinkers and a slow number was oozing from the stereo and he was dancing with her up close, he whispered in her ear that part of him was sorry, the part that was alive, the part that hadn't died. And she shifted the position of her head on his shoulder to let him know she had heard. And the moment had come to tell her he wanted to move in with her, how about tonight, I could get my stuff tomorrow or the day after . . . but as he brought his mouth close to her ear to whisper he noticed MacRae smiling to him over Helen Aitken's shoulder. Paul Haggerty was doing the same over Cathy Lyon's shoulder. Hugh Mitchell and Graham Pearson were having a long, involved, drunken conversation about teaching and Grogan was sitting alone in the corner, feet splayed apart, a glass of whisky in his hand. He raised it as if to propose a toast and declaimed:

'Scotland is a state of mind.' He drank. 'But if it is a state of mind, it can change.' He drank again. 'And if it can change, it must change.' He drank again. 'And if it must change . . . how are we to change it?' He drained the glass and set it down.

Though everyone seemed to have heard what Grogan had said, no one made any response. Grogan stood up and walked unsteadily to McCoy and Yvonne. He wrapped his arms around the both of them and said: 'Do yourself, Pat, do yourself.'

'He's trying,' said Yvonne.

Grogan staggered to the doorway, turned and held a hand up to say goodbye. He swayed there, one hand in the air, trapped in his leavetaking.

McCoy looked around the room and took it all in, as if to fix it in his memory, a night to remember, the New Year he had died, then he wondered what it would really be like to be nobody, nobody else, nobody not himself, as the three couples circled around each other slowly and the dawn light began to show through the curtains.

It was the first day of the year.